The closer she came, the more Patrick saw something different on her face—something softer.

Christie's lips curved to a shy smile and he relaxed.

"I came by to thank you for the flowers. They're beautiful," she said.

"I'm glad you like them," he said. "I recalled how much you loved flowers. I used to surprise you with them. Remember?"

A strand of hair had drifted from behind her ear and caught on her cheek. Patrick longed to reach over and brush it from her face.

"I remember," she said.

A look filled her eyes, sparking a heady sensation through his chest. He searched her face, wanting to tell her so much—how pretty she was and how sorry he felt about the past. He wanted her to know about his faith.

Books by Gail Gaymer Martin

Steeple Hill Single Title

The Christmas Kite

Love Inspired

Upon a Midnight Clear #117
Secrets of the Heart #147
A Love for Safekeeping #161
Loving Treasures #177
Loving Hearts #199
"The Butterfly Garden"/*Easter Blessings* #202
"All Good Gifts"/*The Harvest* #223
Loving Ways #231
Loving Care #239

GAIL GAYMER MARTIN

loves life. She adores her husband, family, writing, singing, traveling and her Lord. With all those blessings, God gave her one more gift—her dream of writing novels. Gail is a multipublished author in nonfiction and fiction with seventeen novels, six novellas and many more to come. Her Steeple Hill Love Inspired romances, *Upon a Midnight Clear,* and *Loving Treasures* won Holt Medallions in 2001 and 2003 respectively, and *A Love for Safekeeping* won the ACRW 2002 Book of the Year Award in short contemporary.

Besides writing, Gail travels across the country guest speaking and presenting workshops for writers. She lives in Lathrup Village, with Bob—her husband and her best friend.

She loves to hear from her readers. Write to her at P.O. Box 760063, Lathrup Village, MI 48076 and visit her Web site, www.gailmartin.com.

LOVING
CARE

GAIL GAYMER MARTIN

Published by Steeple Hill Books™

STEEPLE HILL BOOKS

Steeple
Hill®

ISBN 0-373-87249-6

LOVING CARE

Copyright © 2004 by Gail Gaymer Martin

Visit us at www.steeplehill.com

Printed in U.S.A.

"For He is our God and we are the people of His pasture, the flock under His care."
                                              —*Psalms* 95:7

To my husband, Bob,
who's made all my dreams come true.
I could love you no deeper or surer.
Thank you for all the sacrifices you make for me.

Chapter One

Patrick.

Christie Hanuman's heart almost stopped. She turned her head to avoid eye contact and studied the display of plastic strip bandages.

Her hands trembled as she selected a couple of packages with cartoon figures and dropped them into the basket. Near the bottom of the display, another of the children's favorite designs caught her attention, and she reached for it, wanting to finish her shopping and get out of the store before...

"Christie?"

Hearing his voice, Christie jerked, and the boxes tumbled from the shelves with a domino effect, falling in a heap at her feet as she spun around to face him.

Time had improved his good looks. Age had perfected his tall, lean body, broadening his chest and filling out his shoulders. Even the new facial creases added character to his strong features.

She struggled to calm herself while panic set in her lungs. She maneuvered her facial muscles into a pleasant expression.

Voice don't fail me now.

"What are you doing in town, Patrick?" She relaxed, hearing her tone sound steady and natural.

"I...my dad hasn't been well." He glanced toward the heap of boxes around her feet and dug his hands into his pockets. "He's asked me to..."

Christie watched his Adam's apple rise and fall as he swallowed.

"...take over the hardware business."

The information rolled over her like an eighteen-wheeler. "You mean...you're moving back to Loving?" Holding her breath, she waited for his response while tension rose up her back.

He gave her a slow nod. "We're staying with Dad for now." He slipped one hand from his pocket and ran it over his hair. "If he's doing okay, I'll look for a place."

His plans sounded way too permanent for Christie.

"Otherwise..." He shrugged, and his eyes filled with tenderness.

Christie recalled the gentle look he once used with her, and the memory rattled her. She clutched her shoulder bag, fearing her trembling hands might give her away.

"If he needs me," he continued, "we'll have to stay with Dad."

We'll. Patrick and his wife. Christie had heard about his marriage, but hearing about it when he'd been away had been one thing. Seeing him now was another.

Christie hated the emotion that rushed through her. She stumbled backward and felt her heel sink into one of the plastic strip packages. "I hope your dad's doing better soon," she mumbled, wishing to sound sincere. In reality, she didn't know how she felt as her emotions fluttered and thudded through her like captured birds.

"Thanks." Patrick tucked his hands into his jeans pocket again and jingled his coins a moment, then pulled them out. He seemed as edgy as she felt. His gaze dropped again toward the floor and the pile at her feet.

"Dad has his good days," he said. He bent down and retrieved the crushed plastic strip package, pushing it back into shape. "But handling the business full-time is too strenuous for him now." He shoved the box onto the shelf, then crouched again.

Having no clue what to say next, Christie knelt beside him. As they reached for the same package, his hand brushed hers, and she held her breath. Why did he have to come back to Loving? Why now, when she'd gotten her life organized, and she'd managed to get her day-care center off the ground and thriving?

He rose first and jammed the boxes onto the shelves. Christie straightened and waited. When he'd finished, she added hers and rearranged them into two neat rows. Now that Patrick had returned to jumble up her life, she wondered if things could ever be as orderly again.

He stood beside her without speaking until she'd finished.

"How have you been, Christie?" Patrick asked.

The seeds of revenge shot through her heart. His question had unlocked a door that sent her pride marching forward with a flag of victory. "I've opened a day-care center." She managed to hold a direct gaze.

His face paled, it seemed, with a tinge of remembrance. His full lips pressed together until the color faded to white, but he appeared to rally and drew himself upward. "Good for you."

She scrutinized his statement. His voice sounded too loud and overly sincere. She guessed he hated her for reaching her goal without his direction. Hated her success. "A child-care center was always my dream."

"I remember," he said.

This time the noticeable regret in his voice surprised her.

"The business is doing well," she said. "Very well."

"I never thought it wouldn't. When you have a goal, it never fails."

It never fails. The words stabbed her. The one thing most important to her had failed. Their marriage. "Not everything, Patrick." Her verbal knife twisted, and she watched his face wrench through a series of emotions.

"Well, most things," he said, with a faint shrug.

Seeing his reaction, Christie wished she could retract her words. Patrick's chocolate-brown eyes grew dark, and his handsome face appeared as strained as she felt. "I'm sorry. No sense dragging out the past," she said.

"I don't blame you," he said, taking a step back, his attention drawn to the display of bandage strips.

"Thanks for helping me put back the boxes," she said.

"No problem."

His gaze caught hers, and she felt her pulse quicken before he looked away.

"I only wish…" His voice faded as if dealing with an unspoken regret, but he recovered and smiled. "Anyway, congratulations on the business. I'd love to see it sometime."

"Thanks." She avoided responding to his request. Why did he want to see the center? She could only imagine he would find fault with it. Nitpick. Patrick had always needed to be in charge, but she noticed he still couldn't make a neat row with the boxes.

He opened his mouth, then closed it as if he'd wanted to say something.

Though Christie recognized disappointment in his face, she had no desire to appease him. She hadn't been able to please him years earlier. Why try now? She stepped backward, stretching the distance between them. "I imagine I'll see you around."

"I'm sure," he said, lifting his hand in a feeble farewell.

She turned and headed for the checkout. No way would she continue shopping and run into him again in another aisle. Seeing him today had reopened the wound she'd soothed and healed years ago. She looked at the packages of plastic strips in her basket and wondered which one she should use to cover the deep scar that ached within her.

Patrick watched Christie leave. She was as lovely as he remembered—bright and pretty as a spring flower. Yet, as always, he'd been pricked by the bee that lived inside those graceful petals. He remembered the sting all too well.

Remorse washed over him as he watched her vanish through the doorway, and his mind clouded as to why he'd come to the pharmacy to begin with. Then he remembered. To pick up his father's heart medication. He headed toward the pharmacist, and when he caught his attention, the man came to the counter.

"I'm picking up my dad's prescription. Joe Hanuman."

The man adjusted his glasses and took a long look before he responded. "Patrick?"

Patrick smiled. "It's been a long time, Mr. Levin."

"Why, it sure has." Levin stepped away and returned in a moment with two pill bottles. "Your dad mentioned you'd be coming home to give him a hand."

Patrick could only nod. He'd pried himself away from his own career and uprooted his life, but his father had been a good parent—a single parent—and he could never fault him for a few flaws.

"I heard about your loss, Patrick." He reached beneath the counter and pulled out a white bag detailed with a prescription logo on the front.

"Thanks. It's been rough at times."

"God doesn't give you anything you can't handle," the pharmacist said, handing Patrick the package.

The man's voice filled with sorrow, and Patrick recalled Mr. Levin's wife had been ill for years—something serious, but he couldn't recall what.

"How's your boy doing?" Levin asked.

"Growing like a weed. He's three now." Since he'd run into Christie, Patrick had lost all direction, and Levin's question served as a reminder. He raised a finger. "Hang on a minute." He hurried to a display of inexpensive toys and selected two miniature cars packaged together, then returned to the counter. "Think this is too grown-up for him?" His lack of confidence as a parent grated on him.

"Naw. Boys like anything that has a motor." He gave Patrick a grin. "That'll be..." He punched the register and hit the total. "Nine-thirteen."

Patrick handed him a ten.

Levin counted out the change. "Tell your dad I send my best wishes."

"I'll do that, and thanks." Patrick slid the change into his pocket, grasped his purchases and headed for the door, his mind whirring.

Outside, the bright June sun shimmered off the cars parked in front. As always in Michigan, the humidity in summer weighted the air. Patrick pulled out his keys, unlocked his car door and slid inside. He dropped the package on the passenger seat and sat a moment, rubbing his face with both hands.

Images of Christie clogged his mind. He needed to talk with her. He didn't know if she'd heard he'd gotten married. She hadn't said anything today, but harder still was telling her about Sean.

He reached down and turned the key in the ignition, admitting to himself it was only right he tell Christie about Sherry and Sean before someone else did. Christie had been an important part of his life once, and he owed her the truth—at least as much as he had the courage to reveal.

Patrick pulled into the driveway, glad to be home. He hadn't left Sean with his father before, and at times, the boy could be a handful, getting into everything, but Patrick's father insisted he could meet the challenge.

In the living room, he set the medicine bottles beside his father's recliner and listened to the silence. His heart skipped a beat. Where were they? He shouldn't have left Sean alone with his father. Another unthinking decision he'd made. He searched, and finding the first-floor rooms empty, he climbed the stairs and hurried down the hallway, fear in his chest.

When Patrick saw them, his pulse slowed and calmed. Grandpa and Sean were curled together on the bed, asleep. He could hear his father's steady breathing and see the rise and fall of Sean's small chest. As Patrick stood in the doorway, love filled his heart. Love for his tiny son and love for a father who'd done his best. The paradox struck him. He'd been raised by his father, and now he was raising his son…alone. An awesome task, he realized each day as he tried to earn a living and meet his son's needs.

Sometimes he asked God why. Why had He taken his wife away so young? Why had Patrick been forced to be a single parent like his father? Hadn't he had enough, growing up alone, wanting a mother so badly?

Patrick leaned against the bedroom doorjamb, reeling with memories Christie had stirred—memories he'd tried so hard to keep locked away. With a final look at his father and his son, Patrick pushed his back from the doorframe and stepped into the hallway.

"You back already?" his father whispered.

Patrick chuckled. "I've been gone over an hour."

His dad rubbed his eyes and slipped out from under Sean's arm. "Had to do something to get this boy to take a nap."

Patrick observed the pleasure on his father's face, and, if nothing more, he felt happy he could make his father's difficult days a little brighter…and a lot more lively.

Joe gave a wide stretch, hoisted his pants and slid his feet into well-worn slippers, then followed Patrick from the bedroom.

"I hate to leave him up here without one of us," Patrick said. "He could fall down the stairs."

"No, he can't." Joe opened the hall closet and pulled out a safety gate. "I planned ahead. Everything's put away up here, and he'll let us know when he wakes. If you move him now, he'll wake up crabby, and then you'll really have your hands full."

While his father fumbled with the gate, Patrick pondered whether he was making a wise choice. Still, his dad was right. Sean would let them know he wanted company as soon as he woke.

"Need help with that?" Patrick asked.

"Let me do one thing I can handle, son. I don't have many of those opportunities anymore."

Patrick nodded and breathed more easily as he took the steps down to the first floor. He found it hard not to take over every task, but he needed to leave his dad some dignity and some sense of independence.

Downstairs, Patrick headed for the kitchen to grab something for lunch before he left for the hardware store. When he heard his father's footsteps, Patrick called over his shoulder. "Want a sandwich, Dad?"

His father shuffled through the doorway and gazed at the clock. "By jingo, I did sleep a while. It's past lunch time." He went to the bread bag and pulled out a couple of slices. "Slap some meat on this for me if you don't mind."

Patrick did as he'd asked and slipped the sandwich onto a paper plate. While his father bit into the bread without remembering to pray, Patrick lowered his head and said a silent blessing. Though he'd been raised without religion, for some reason in recent years, his father had begun to attend church. Patrick, too, had come to know God's saving grace as an adult—years after he'd divorced Christie. He didn't know if his mother had been a believer or not.

"Why so quiet?" Joe asked, a blob of mayo clinging to his lip.

Patrick pointed, and his dad pulled a napkin from the holder and wiped his mouth. "Nothing particular. Just thinking."

His dad raised an eyebrow and gave him a steady look. "Did you get my medicine?"

Patrick nodded. "It's by your recliner." The words struck him. Times like this he missed Sherry—a woman in his life, a mother with common sense for his son. "I suppose I should put it away before Sean gets into it. I wasn't thinking."

"You better start thinking, boy. That little one is precious."

Drawing a deep breath, Patrick nodded, angry at himself for being so careless. "You're right, Dad. I'm distracted."

His father wiped his mouth again and drew back his head, eyeing Patrick from beneath knitted eyebrows. "What's bothering you, Patrick? You've been my son for a long time. I know when you've got something on your mind."

Patrick never could hide anything from his father. He'd hoped to avoid talking about Christie, but the same facial expression that had gotten him in trouble as a child was doing it again.

He dropped his half-eaten sandwich onto the paper plate. "I ran into Christie today at the pharmacy."

"Christie."

"Right. It just threw me off-kilter a little."

His father leaned one elbow on the table and rubbed the side of his head. "Was she civil?"

"She was surprised to see me, but she acted fine. Told me about her child-care business." Patrick broke eye contact and turned his plate ninety degrees, then pulled it back. "That bothered me."

"Why?"

He shook his head. "She'd wanted to run her own center when we were married. I…I asked her to wait until we were financially stable."

Joe nodded. "Yes. I remember that. So what is it then. Did she say something about Sherry or Sean?"

Patrick's stomach knotted around the piece of bread and meat he'd eaten. "I don't know if she knows about them."

"You mean you didn't tell her?"

"I didn't say anything. It wasn't a good time."

"You're not ashamed of your son, are you?"

His father's words struck Patrick like a knife. "How can you ask that?" But looking at his father's face, he sensed his answer. Christie didn't hesitate to let him know about her success…and with pride. He'd cowered, fearing to mention his son.

His father's question had struck a heavy blow. He could have mentioned that his son was also staying at his father's. He could have said more…even about his wife's death. Why hadn't he? Instead, he'd avoided mentioning it as if he were ashamed.

"This is a small town. Gossip flies like a house afire," his father said. "If she doesn't know already, then you need to—"

"I know, Dad." His thoughts whirred while unexpected visions rose in Patrick's mind—Christie sitting by the firelight when they went camping,

Christie picking wildflowers in a spring meadow, Christie laughing, with the wind blowing her honey-brown hair. The images rolled over him like waves on a beach. "I owe her the decency of telling her myself…and I will."

His father's eyes narrowed. "Okay." He shoved the paper plate away from him. "When?"

Chapter Two

Christie slid the blueprint around so she could look at it more carefully. "I'd like to have more storage space in this area." She pointed to the spot on the proposed floor plan for the day-care-center addition. She'd been contemplating the changes for months. She demanded perfection.

"Storage, huh?" The builder studied the drawing again.

The telephone jingled, and Christie paused to see if one of her assistants would grab it. When it rang a third time, she excused herself and crossed the room to her desk. "Loving Care."

"Christie, this is Patrick."

Christie's chest tightened. A week had passed since she'd seen him. She gripped the receiver, pulling it close to her mouth to keep her voice from reaching the man standing by her worktable. "What do you want, Patrick?" The cross words flew from her, but she didn't care, assuming Patrick was pushing to see the day-care facility. Seeing him hurt too badly. When he walked out on their marriage, she'd struggled to make her life meaningful. She couldn't do it again.

For a moment, only silence seeped across the line. Finally he spoke. "I thought we…I wondered if we could talk. I—"

"I'm sorry, Patrick. This is a bad time for me. I'm very busy." Realizing her volume had risen, she lowered her voice. "And I don't see what we have to talk about. We talked eight years ago." Her knees had begun to shake, and she felt light-headed. She longed to sit, but she felt the contractor's eyes on her back so she fought to remain calm.

"Yes, I know, but…" His voice faded to resignation for a moment. With a new fervor, he continued. "I'll try again when you're not so busy. Sorry I bothered you."

When Christie realized he'd hung up, she lowered the telephone and closed her eyes. His voice had sparked with anger, and she felt riddled with regret. What had happened to her clear thinking? Her control?

Having Patrick back in town threw her off course enough. Talking to him, rehashing the past seemed useless and could only stir up emotions she'd packed away.

Managing a pleasant look, Christie spun around to face the contractor. "So, where were we?" she asked, crossing the room to the worktable.

He tapped the blueprint. "You asked about storage."

"Yes," she said, struggling to keep focused.

"I think we could shave a little off this new playroom." The contractor ran his finger along the line of an imaginary wall. "Or we could add some built-ins here. Large shelves maybe along this wall and some benches under these windows. You know, the kind that serve as storage chests."

"Benches? I like that idea."

"So?" The contractor tapped his foot as she perused the blueprint. "What do you think?"

"I like what I see. At least, with the changes. I would still have plenty of room for the children's outside play, and—" Her heart sank as she realized since Patrick's call she'd lost interest in talking about an addition.

"I'll tell you what," she said. "Let me study the drawings for a few days. If I decide to go through with this, I'll check with my bank for a loan approval."

She noticed a concerned twist to his face.

"I'll have no trouble getting approval," she added to assure him, "but I need to be confident I'm moving in the right direction."

"Certainly," he said, regaining his salesman's smile. He did a full turn looking around her office.

"You have a nice facility here. You might as well make it the best you can, and we're just the company that can bring your dream to life."

Christie had heard that line before, but she shook his hand and smiled. When he vanished through the door, her pleasant expression faded. She left her copy of the blueprint on the table and was heading for her desk when the telephone rang again. Patrick. She grabbed the receiver.

"Loving Care," she said, controlling her tone, yet wondering if Patrick would ever give up.

"Christie, this is Milton." His voice held a question. "Are you okay?"

"Sorry, Milton. I'm just busy." She massaged her forehead with her free hand, angry at her loss of composure.

"I won't keep you. I just wanted to make sure we're still on for tonight."

She sank into her chair. "How could I forget? Sure we're on."

"Good. I'll pick you up around seven-thirty."

"See you then," she said, determined not to let Patrick's reappearance mess up her life.

When she'd hung up, Christie kept her fingers wrapped around the receiver and thought. Despite her decision to remain single, she'd found the company of men pleasurable, and Milton Garrison had accepted her rules—a date was nothing more than companionship. But she didn't love him. She'd only ever loved one man—Patrick.

Patrick. Had she been unfair to him today? Maybe she should phone him back and apologize for her brusque treatment. She stared into space.

Stupid idea. I owe him nothing, and all he wants is to ease his guilt.

But was that all? The more she pondered, the more her curiosity took over her thoughts. He wanted to talk, he'd said, but what did he want really?

More important, what did she want really?

Christie placed her knife along the edge of the plate and pushed it aside. She hadn't felt hungry, and she'd let Milton do most of the talking through dinner. She could tell by his expression he wondered what was wrong. She managed to brighten her smile and look interested. "You didn't tell me how your meetings went."

His attention sharpened, and he gave her a faint smile. "They went well. Sorry I had to be out of town last weekend." He slid his hand across the table to brush her arm. "I hope that didn't upset you. I missed you."

He'd thought she was upset with him, Christie realized. She knew she should say she missed him, too, but she hadn't. Since she'd run into Patrick on Saturday afternoon, followed by his telephone call, the next week, she hadn't thought about anyone else. Instead of telling a lie, she smiled and patted Milton's hand resting on her arm.

"I'm glad the meetings were worthwhile," she said.

He looked thoughtful and nodded.

Christie grappled for conversation. "By the way, I met with a contractor from Jeffers Construction today. He brought over the blueprints."

His eyes widened, and a look of interest replaced his dour expression. "And what do you think?"

She heard him, but something had drawn her attention to the dining-room entrance. Heat rose up her neck as she spotted Patrick standing in the doorway waiting for the hostess. When the woman guided him to a table nearby, Christie cringed. Discomfort rattled her, and she felt like a woman cheating on her husband.

"Is something wrong?"

She shifted her gaze to Milton, yet in her peripheral vision, she could tell Patrick had seen her. Moments passed before his question settled in her ears.

"Sorry. Nothing's wrong." She managed a grin and took a sip of her ice water, hoping she wouldn't get sick right there in the restaurant.

"I asked you what you thought of the blueprints?" Milton's forehead creased as he studied her.

"Oh...the blueprints. Yes. Good. They looked pretty good. I made a couple of suggestions."

Milton glanced over his shoulder as if searching for what had caused her distraction. When he turned back, he was unsmiling. "Do you know that man?"

Christie nodded. "It's Patrick."

He glanced again. "You mean *your* Patrick."

"Yes. No. Not *my* Patrick. Not now, but he used to be." She kept her eyes directed at Milton, struggling with what to do with Patrick so near. Speak to him. Ignore him.

"Would you like to leave?" Milton asked, his curiosity switching to a look of irritation.

"No. Not at all." In truth, Christie longed to run. She and Milton had been dating for many months, a year maybe, and today she wanted to hide their relationship. She resented the feeling and felt frustrated for reacting that way.

She tried to pretend she didn't know Patrick was there, but her conversation lagged worse than before while her mind filled with questions. Where was his wife? Why had he come to this restaurant? And why tonight? It had been one of her favorites. He shouldn't have come here.

The thought plagued her. Why had *she* come here? He had every right to eat here. Patrick had loved the place as much as she had. It had been their special restaurant—the one they'd come to during one of their college breaks when he'd first told her he loved her.

"I should speak to him, I suppose," Christie said.

Milton tilted his head. "I'm guessing you mean Patrick."

Mortified that she'd blurted out her thoughts

aloud, she nodded. "Sorry. Seeing him here surprised me."

"You didn't know he was in town?" Milton asked.

"I did, actually. We ran into each other at the pharmacy on Saturday." She swallowed, knowing she had to be candid. "He's come back to town...to stay."

A shadow fell across Milton's face, and his look darkened. "You mean to live?"

She gave a faint nod. "His dad's ill. Hanuman's Hardware belongs to his father, and he needs Patrick's help." Christie realized for the first time that she hadn't even asked Patrick what was wrong with his dad.

Milton pushed his plate aside and twisted in the chair to flag the waitress.

Knowing that she'd dampened his mood and ruined his meal, Christie wished she could backtrack and choose another place for their dinner. Why had she picked Anton's Bistro tonight of all nights?

The waitress came, and Milton paid the check. He gave Christie a nod and stood to assist her rising. She slung her bag over her shoulder, and when she turned, her gaze riveted to Patrick's.

"Hello," she said, feeling more awkward than she had since being a teenager. "Patrick, this is my friend, Milton Garrison."

Patrick slid back his chair and rose, the cloth napkin dangling from his fingers. He grasped Milton's outstretched hand with a steady shake. "Nice to meet you." He shifted his gaze to Christie. "Did you enjoy your dinner?"

"Yes, I did." *Before you came in,* she added as she felt her food churn in her stomach.

"We always liked Anton's," Patrick said, his narrowed gaze not shifting from hers.

With his last pointed comment, she unleashed her question. "Where's your wife, Patrick? I heard you were married."

His face drained of color, and she realized too late she'd stepped on sensitive ground.

"Sherry died a couple of years ago."

"Died? Oh, Patrick, I'm so sorry. I hadn't heard. I—I didn't know."

"It was sudden."

Words failed her, and Christie felt the pressure of Milton's fingers against her arm, urging her toward the door. "We need to get going, Patrick." Her voice trailed away, longing to tell him how sorry she was, not only at his wife's death, but at her tactless question.

"See you around," he said, sliding back into his chair and draping the napkin across his lap before he scooted forward.

"See you," she said, moving away on Milton's tense arm.

"Look, Ellie," Christie said, nestling the two year old in her arms. She pointed to the sky. "See all the kites."

"See da kites," Ellie mimicked.

"Jemma," Christie said, "your daughter talks better than some of my three-year olds at the day care."

Jemma Somerville grinned. "She takes after her daddy."

"Daddy," Ellie said, twisting her body to search the crowd at the Grand Haven Paint the Sky Kite Fly.

"Your daddy's working," Christie said, nuzzling the child's rosy cheeks. "Thanks for inviting me to come along, Jemma. The kites are beautiful."

Ellie wiggled in Christie's arms.

"You want down, sweetie?" Christie asked. She lowered the toddler to the ground but gripped her hand so she wouldn't wander off.

"Let Mommy tie your shoe," Jemma said, crouching to redo the child's laces. "You'll be falling on your face if we aren't careful."

While Christie waited beside them, she lifted her head toward the sunny sky, admiring the shapes and colors dipping and soaring on the breeze. She loved feeling summer's warmth on her skin. The smell of Lake Michigan tantalized her senses along with the nearby food booths that tempted her palate.

She turned toward the stands to check the length of the lines. Her breath halted. Patrick. Again. His dark hair and broad shoulders stood out from the crowd as he waited at an ice-cream concession. She gazed at his profile while an unwanted sensation rippled along her spine. She'd always known he was handsome, but now he'd ripened like a summer peach—rosy tan from the sun and so tempting.

Washed in unexpected feelings, she shifted her gaze and noticed a boy—three years old, she guessed—standing beside him. The child's dark hair and the same sculpted nose sent her heart on a downward plunge.

"What's wrong?" Jemma asked as she rose from the shoe-tying. She turned to look in the direction that Christie's gaze had frozen.

"Patrick's over there by the ice-cream stand."

"Which one is he?"

"With the dark hair and—"

Jemma touched her arm. "You mean the good-looking man with the child?"

Christie swallowed. "Right. The good-looking one."

"Is the boy his?" Jemma asked.

Distraught, Christie shrugged. "I'm guessing he is."

"He never told you?"

She gave a single shake of her head while anger and envy pelted her.

Jemma's arm slid around Christie's shoulders with a quick embrace. "You could be wrong. The boy could be a relative...or neighbor." She nudged Christie forward. "Talk with him."

"I can't."

"Ice cream," Ellie called, her arm, straight as an arrow, pointing to the booth. "Ice cream, Mommy."

"Ellie wants a treat. Let's go over there," Jemma said, lifting Ellie in her arms and stepping ahead before Christie could stop her.

Christie waited a moment, not wanting to move, not wanting to learn the truth, but Jemma flagged her forward and she followed against her will.

As Christie approached, Patrick was handing a small cone to the young boy. As he straightened, he saw her. His flustered glance at the child validated her guilty verdict. Christie had no question that the boy was his, and the closer she came, the more she recognized the child's large brown eyes, so like his father's.

"Hello, Patrick." Before she let him respond, Christie shifted her attention to the boy. "Are you enjoying the kites?"

"That one," the child said, pointing toward a box kite with multicolored sides bobbing in the air.

"That's a nice one," Christie said, unable to take her gaze from the boy. She'd seen pictures of Patrick when he was young and the child looked identical, except for his chin which seemed more peaked and lacked the hint of a dimple.

Patrick rested his hand on the child's shoulder. "Christie, this is my son, Sean." He sighed. "That's why I wanted to talk with—"

"Hi, Sean." Christie kept her back turned. She

didn't want to hear the rest. She'd longed for a child throughout their seven-year marriage, but he'd opposed it. *Wait until we're settled. Wait until we have a bigger house. Wait until we have savings. Wait. Wait. Wait.* Her life had been on hold, waiting for some undefinable goal that Patrick had firmly established.

The boy grinned at her, his eyes twinkling with curiosity. "Who are you?"

"Your daddy's...old friend." The word *daddy* wrenched her heart. Patrick with a son. Christie, childless.

The boy stared at her as he licked the edge of his cone.

"How's your father, Patrick? I didn't ask what's wrong when we spoke before."

"His heart. He's had a couple of minor attacks. They've taken a toll on him."

"I'm sorry to hear that," Christie said.

"Thanks."

Christie glanced over her shoulder to search for Jemma. She spotted her beside Ellie, holding an ice cream and catching the chocolate as it ran down her fingers. The unmerciful sun made eating the treat a challenge.

When Christie looked back, Sean was stopping a drip of his own while Patrick clasped a soggy cone holding untouched ice cream. A look of sadness had replaced his discomfort, arousing a new feeling in

Christie. Her self-pity faded to compassion. Patrick was raising the child alone.

Swallowing her prideful indignation, Christie tilted her head toward the boy. "This must be difficult."

He shrugged. "At times, but a gift, too." His eyes searched hers. "If I'd only known years ago—"

She raised her hand. "It's too late for that." Too late. The meaning pressed against her heart until it ached.

Jemma had moved closer, and when Christie noticed, she beckoned her to join them. "Patrick, I don't think you know Jemma Somerville. Her husband owns Bay Breeze Resort." She reached down to fondle Ellie's head. "And this is Ellie. She's one of my day-care children."

Addled by the situation, Christie remembered the young boy. "Jemma, this is Sean, Patrick's son." Her voice caught in her throat.

Jemma greeted the child, then shook hands with Patrick, and when he knelt down to speak with Ellie, Jemma mouthed her concern. "Are you all right?"

Christie sent her a private look to indicate she was okay. But she wasn't. Her heart felt crushed, and she wanted to pummel Patrick's chest, to stomp her foot and demand her rights.

Rights? She had every right to have her own child. Milton had hinted at marriage more than once, but she'd steered him away from the topic, determined to remain single. Had she made a mistake?

She could change her way of thinking and become Mrs. Milton Garrison. Maybe that's what she needed to do despite her beliefs that God did not bless a marriage after a divorce.

Patrick hadn't noticed until too late that his ice cream had tilted on the cone. The melting glob slipped from its housing and dropped to the ground. "I didn't want it anyway," he said, shaking his head and pulling another napkin from his pocket to mop the mess from his hands, then retrieved the fallen glob and tossed it all into a nearby waste basket.

"Sorry," Christie said, feeling responsible for the mishap.

"Not your fault," he said.

Christie grasped Ellie's hand, a defensive move on her part, she realized, but she needed to feel motherly and loved. "We'd better let you go."

"Oh…then, I'll call you sometime," Patrick said as they moved away.

"Sure," she said, wanting to say no, but how could she? He had every right to come back to Loving, and she'd have to learn to live with it.

Chapter Three

Wednesday, Patrick clutched the inventory clipboard and tallied the rows of hammers. He felt as if he'd been hit in the head with one since seeing Christie at the restaurant a little more than a week ago. The image glared in his memory. Christie with another man. Patrick had no cause for jealousy, but he couldn't explain his feelings except pure rivalry. He didn't want Christie with another man.

Next had come the Kite Fly. That had added to his misery. His head pounded; and he'd not been able to ease the stress since that afternoon. In the past two days, he'd snapped at Sean without thinking and ripped at his father for forgetting to take his medicine. He'd done everything but lambaste the person who'd caused him stress. Christie.

If she'd given him her precious time to talk, to

tell her about Sherry and Sean, his son's presence wouldn't have thrown her as it had. He'd seen the expression on her face. Watched the downturn of her mouth as she tried to be civil. She didn't fool him. Not one iota. Christie had a way of turning him off when she wanted to hurt him. That had been their past. He figured she hadn't changed.

Suddenly, Patrick had another recollection—the look on Christie's face when she'd shown her concern. *This must be difficult,* he could still hear her say. Something had caused her to soften. Something had turned her biting tone to a gentler one. He thanked God for that.

He checked his own behavior. He'd been uncomfortable telling her about Sean. How could he allow his feelings for his son to be affected by guilt? Sean had done nothing but be born to brighten his and Sherry's lives. After Sherry's death, he would have fallen apart except for Sean. The boy needed him, and he needed his son.

No matter, he wanted to smooth things with Christie. They lived in the same town. They would meet as they had in the past week or two. He owed her an apology. *Apology.* The words seemed so empty. He owed her much more than that.

"Excuse me."

A voice brought Patrick back from his thoughts and he turned to face the man.

"Could you point me to the three-way plugs?"

"They're right over here," Patrick said, leading

the way. In a few steps, he showed the man the display.

"Thanks." The gentleman turned and extended his hand. "I'm Pastor Tom Myers from United Christian Church. I don't believe we've met."

"Pastor Myers." Patrick took his hand. "My father has spoken of you. I'm Joe Hanuman's son, Patrick."

"Ah. Welcome home, Patrick. Your dad's looked forward to your coming back to Loving." He gave Patrick's shoulder a squeeze. "I hope we'll see you in church."

"If Dad's feeling better, we plan to come this Sunday. He's anxious to get back to church, too."

"Glad to hear it," Pastor Tom said, eyeing the plugs and pulling a couple from the hook. "Before you slip away—" he turned to face Patrick "—my wife asked me to pick up some of that green stuff you use to arrange flowers. You know, you can shove the stems right—"

"Oasis." Patrick grinned at the man's description. "It's in the gardening department. Let me show you."

"No need. Thanks. I'll find it myself." Pastor Tom turned away while Patrick's mind resettled on Christie and something the man had said that had triggered a brilliant idea. Flowers. Christie loved them, and a bouquet might be just the thing to soften the tension between them.

He looked down the aisle toward the retreating

clergyman and thanked God the man had needed Oasis. If anything could open the door with Christie, it would be a floral arrangement...and, without a doubt, the Lord's help.

While Christie shuffled papers on her desk at Loving Care, footsteps caused her to lift her head. Annie Dewitt came through the doorway carrying a bouquet wrapped in florist paper.

"This just arrived," Annie said. "Is today your birthday? I'm sorry I didn't—"

"It's not my birthday," Christie said, eyeing the wrapper. "It's from Milton or Jeffers Construction, I'll bet. They'll do anything to get someone to sign on the dotted line." But in the back of her mind, Christie guessed the flowers were from Milton, remembering how upset he'd been the day he'd met Patrick.

Annie waited while Christie peeled back the paper.

As soon as she made an opening, a sweet scent escaped the wrapping. Christie peeked inside and eyed the colorful mixed bouquet, too beautiful and expensive to be from a builder trying to beguile a customer.

"There's the card," Annie said, pointing to the square envelope on a plastic card holder sticking up through the blossoms.

"Hold these," Christie said, handing Annie the lovely arrangement while she pulled the card from the paper jacket. She stared at the message, allowing time for reality to settle in.

"I was wrong," Christie said, feeling her pulse pick up speed.

"Then who?"

"Patrick."

"Your ex?"

Nodding, Christie released a weighty sigh and studied the large bouquet. "I don't know what I'm going to do, Annie."

"What do you mean?"

Christie handed her the card and waited while she skimmed the note.

"He's just asking to talk with you. That can't hurt, can it?" She returned the card to Christie, then crossed to the desk, pulled off the rest of the florist paper, and placed the bouquet on the corner.

Could it hurt? Christie had finally overcome those earlier years. She'd struggled to regain her feelings of self-worth, and though she'd tried to understand what had happened, she'd failed. Nothing had come to help her understand why Patrick had faced her one day to say he wanted out of the marriage.

"It's complicated." Adamant about her privacy, Christie broke her rules and gave Annie a sketchy picture of the situation.

"You didn't know he had a child?" Annie's expression showed her surprise.

"No. I wouldn't have known he'd married if my mom hadn't heard the news. The grapevine must have lost interest in Patrick since his wedding. That's the last I heard."

"I'm sure it hurts," Annie said. "Wanting a child for so long and then…" She shook her head, her eyes downcast, her face reflecting a deep-felt emotion. When she lifted her gaze, a renewed spirit lit her eyes. "But you can't let it hold you back from living your life. Look at Ken and me. We're in our forties and adopting a child. But you. You're young enough to marry and have kids of your own. It's not like you don't date. I'm sure Milton would give his—"

"I can't remarry, Annie, even if I wanted to. I realize I haven't been a good Christian these past years. I've been angry at God for what happened, but I still believe, and the Bible says, that marriage after divorce is a sin."

Silent, Annie stared at her a moment. "I don't know what to say."

Her voice faded with the same hopeless feeling Christie had felt for years as she clung to that belief, despite her longing to be a mother. The day care had provided a weak facsimile to parenthood.

"What about Patrick?" Annie asked. "He married again."

"Patrick's never been a believer. Without faith, he didn't follow God's rules or anyone's, for that matter. He followed his own."

Hearing her bitter words, Christie shook her head. "I shouldn't have said that. I'm making Patrick sound like an ogre, and he's not. I loved him once. More than I can say.''

Christie quieted, uncomfortable with the disclosure she'd made. When she'd calmed herself, another problem shot through her mind—a problem that had rattled her since she'd learned the truth. ''Being a mother is just about impossible for me anyway. I have endometriosis of all things. It's difficult for me to get pregnant, and I've waited so long now...''

Annie's expression drooped to dismay before she rallied. She wrapped her arm around Christie's shoulders and gave her a squeeze. ''But remember, with God all things are possible. You know that.''

With God all things are possible. Christie wondered. Images darted through her head, images of wonderful days when she and Patrick were young and in love. ''I want to be happy for Patrick. I feel like putty—stretched one way then the other. Patrick seems like a good father, and the child is bright and has Patrick's good looks and sparkling eyes.''

Annie grinned at her. ''And you're still noticing those eyes?''

Her question hit home. ''Me? No. I'm thinking back.'' Christie spotted the questioning look on Annie's smug face and countered. ''Not me, Annie. Never. I can read your mind. I'd never get involved with Patrick again. Never.''

''Never? That's a strong word.''

"I feel strongly about it. I could never trust him again."

"But you could be friends. You live in a small town. And you could forgive him for the past. Remember, God says if we want to be forgiven we must forgive."

"Don't talk about forgiveness." She felt her shoulders stiffen and fire burn in her heart. She liked Annie. She'd become a good, trusting friend, and Annie had gone through difficult times, too. But forgiveness?

"Sorry. It's none of my business, I know," Annie said, taking a step backward as if Christie had slapped her.

Christie chastised herself for the burred remark. "It's not you, Annie. It's just that you don't really understand the situation."

"You're right. I'm sure I don't." Annie checked her watch, then glanced over her shoulder toward the doorway. "I need to help get the kids ready for their parents' arrival before the crew hunts me down." She gave Christie's arm a squeeze and vanished through the doorway.

Forgiveness? Christie closed her eyes. How could she do what the Lord asked? She blamed God as much as Patrick for her problems. Why did she have endometriosis to make things worse? The message seemed loud and clear. She wasn't meant to be a mother. Maybe she would have botched the job. Christie had always believed the Lord could work miracles. She'd prayed to Him day and night to fix her marriage. But God had done nothing to make things better. Neither had Patrick.

Hearing sounds from the front, Christie realized parents were arriving. She put on a pleasant face and headed toward the entrance to greet them.

Parents. Her shoulders lifted as she drew in a calming breath. Patrick was a parent. A single parent. The same way he'd been raised. That had to be difficult.

She pictured his face again as he'd looked at his son that sunny Sunday afternoon at the Kite Fly. The hurt he'd felt from her barbed comments plunged through her thoughts. If she called herself a Christian—even a weak one—she knew she should show compassion. Patrick had asked her to talk. Something so simple. Why couldn't she say okay?

The question sat like a heavy weight in her heart.

Patrick came through the Employees Only doorway and stopped cold. Christie stood near the checkout, talking to one of the clerks. The man's arm raised and pointed toward the door Patrick had just come through, and when Christie's gaze shifted, he realized she saw him.

As she headed his way, Patrick stood still, fearful she would blow her top in the store. He felt for the door behind him. He was near enough to the employee area and could drag her into the stock room if necessary. The image pulled a faint grin to his mouth and eased the tension.

But the closer she came, he saw something different on her face—something softer. Her lips curved to a shy smile and he relaxed.

"Surprised?" she asked.

"Yes," he admitted, realizing his mouth had been gaping. He returned her smile. "I wondered where you were hiding the bat."

"Bat?"

"Baseball bat. To whack me a good one."

She lifted her arms and flexed her wrists front to back. "See. Empty-handed."

"Then why am I so honored?"

"I came by to say thank-you for the flowers. They're beautiful...but totally unnecessary."

"I'm glad you like them." A strand of hair had drifted from behind her ear and caught on her cheek. Patrick longed to reach over and brush it from her face. He recalled its silkiness, the way it slid through his fingers.

A faint frown fell across her eyes and pulled him from his reverie.

"I thought they were necessary," he said.

He sensed her reticence to agree and curbed his desire to offer a lengthy explanation. Now wasn't the time. "I recalled how much you loved flowers. I used to surprise you with them. Remember?"

"I remember," she said.

A look filled her eyes, sparking a heady sensation

through his chest. He glanced around, looking for some place to sit, then pointed toward the door behind him. "Let's go inside where we can have some privacy."

She eyed the door a moment, then fumbled with her shoulder bag. "No. I don't want to take up your time. I was nearby and just wanted to thank you for the flowers."

"I have time, Christie." He searched her eyes, wanting to tell her so much—how pretty she was and how sorry he felt about their failed marriage. He wanted her to know about his faith. There was so much he couldn't say standing here with customers and employees scooting past.

"You look great. Like you did when you were twenty." He let the words glide from his mouth, then noticed a flush rise to her cheeks.

"Don't get sentimental, Patrick. I'm long past twenty. You need to add another fifteen years onto that."

"Look in a mirror," he said.

She gave him a pessimistic frown.

"I'd really like to sit a minute…if you could spare the time." He watched her look turn to a frown. "I think we have some things to clear up."

She took a step backward. "Don't confuse me, Patrick. I know about Sean now. That's what you wanted to tell me. So what do we have to talk about? You have your life, and I've cleared up mine. I've started fresh. My world has order and goals. Talking about old times will only drag out ancient feelings. We don't need that. I'm happy just as I am. Really happy.''

He looked at her sullen face, the misery in her eyes and couldn't stop himself.

''If you're happy, Christie, why aren't you smiling?''

Chapter Four

Christie parked on the street and headed up the walk to her parents' home. She'd promised to drop by, but since seeing Patrick a couple days earlier, she'd been miserable and hadn't felt like talking to anyone.

Patrick's words rang in her ears. *If you're happy, Christie, why aren't you smiling?* She'd wanted to scream in his face that she *was* happy, the happiest she'd ever been, and not only happy but fulfilled. But standing in the middle of a hardware store and screaming how happy she was seemed an act of denial. Instead, she'd ignored his comment.

But had she? The sting ached like a nettle in her skin, swelling and throbbing. How could he be so arrogant? He didn't look happy either, except when he was with his son. When he looked at Sean, Patrick's face glowed with a kind of love she had never known…and never would. The reality pained her.

Christie climbed the steps and turned the doorknob. ''Hi,'' she called, stepping inside.

''I'm in the kitchen,'' her mother answered. ''I'll be through in a minute.''

Christie dropped her shoulder bag on a living-room chair and continued toward her mother's voice. When she came to the doorway, she stopped. ''What are you doing?''

''Scrubbing the floor. What does it look like?'' Emma Goodson brushed a strand of hair from her face and looked up from a kneeling position, a scrub brush clutched in her hand.

''Don't you use a mop?''

''A mop? No. They only slide the dirt around.'' Emma pulled a rag from the bucket, squeezed it and rinsed the floor.

Christie shook her head. ''Mom, you shouldn't be on your knees like that.''

''It's a great time to pray. You should try it.''

Christie sizzled with her mother's words. Back to the old needling about not going to church. She held back a sarcastic response and rested her shoulder against the doorjamb. ''Where's Daddy?''

''He's at the garage getting a tune-up on the car.'' Her mother dropped the brush into a pail and pushed herself up from the floor. She rubbed her hands together as if to dry them and grabbed the bucket.

"Have a seat in the living room, while I get rid of this."

Christie watched her mother tiptoe to the laundry room before turning and doing as she had directed. Taking a moment to gaze through the front picture window, Christie sank into a chair, frustration settling heavily on her emotions.

The battle was unending. In her parents' eyes, she'd never quite grown up. When she and Patrick divorced, she felt as if she'd broken their hearts forever. Still, when she'd returned to Loving and decided to open her own child-care business, they'd been supportive to the point of loaning her money to get started. Despite her irritation, she'd be eternally grateful.

They'd stopped grumbling about the divorce, but they hadn't backed off about church. Not that she didn't believe. She did, but she'd soured after her divorce. Maybe embarrassment kept her away. Perhaps being in church made her feel sinful and displeasing to God. She didn't know which, but attending worship had become a struggle since her marriage ended.

"So," Emma said, coming through the doorway, "did you hear who's back in town?"

Christie gnawed the corner of her lip. "Yes, I ran into him…a couple of times."

"Really?" Emma's eyebrows shot upward as she settled on the sofa.

Christie saw the warning signals in her mother's eyes. "It's a small town, Mom."

"So you know about—"

"His son? Yes. I met him." She gathered her courage and stuck out her chin. "He's the spitting image of Patrick. A good-looking boy."

"Really?"

Concern riddled her mother's face, and Christie knew what was in store—not meanness, just protection.

"I hope you'll use your head about this," Emma said. "Now that he's alone again and with a child, he's probably looking for someone to step in and—"

"I'm not stepping into anything, Mother, so let's drop it."

Her mother's face sagged with Christie's sharp comment, and she wished she could rewrite her last words or at least take the anger out of her voice. "I'm sorry, Mom. It's just that—"

"You don't have to apologize. I know I shouldn't meddle in your life."

"It's a parent's prerogative," Christie said, hoping to smooth over her mother's hurt feelings. "I know you're only trying to protect me from being hurt again."

Emma nodded, fiddling with the hem of her print blouse. "Patrick came from a bad situation. He didn't have a good home life as a boy, and I wonder if he understands the responsibilities of being a husband and father.''

''He looks like a good father to me.'' Christie's defensiveness surprised her. Patrick might not have been the husband he should have been to her, but from all evidence he was a loving father. She had to give him credit.

''Funny,'' Emma said, ''now that Patrick's father has gotten older, we do see him in church once in a while. He must have learned something in his old age. But you still can't forget that grounding comes as a child, and Patrick grew up without Christianity, Christie. He had no guidelines to follow God's bidding. A person without the Lord is shortchanged on the side of righteousness.''

Though she understood her mother's meaning, Christie felt edgy about the statement. She'd been as negligent as Patrick, drifting from church and her faith even though she'd been raised in it. ''Does that mean I don't have morals or integrity because I don't go to church regularly?''

Emma drew back, her eyes widened. ''You? Heavens no. You were brought up to know the Lord. You've slacked off on church, but not on believing.''

Her mother had that right, but Christie wondered sometimes if she'd ever feel the same as she did as a child. Jesus walked with her in those days. Today, her footsteps felt mighty lonely.

''I figured you haven't remarried because you

know what God expects,'' her mother continued. ''Unless Patrick committed adultery, and you said he didn't have another woman when he left you. At least, one you knew about.''

''I believe him, Mom. Patrick left for other reasons. Not another woman. Now, can we change the subject?'' Christie had never understood the reason he left. Not fully anyway, but she'd accept Patrick's denial of another woman. Maybe she'd done that for her own pride, but in her heart, she believed him.

Emma leaned forward. ''I just wanted you to—''

''Hello,'' Wes Goodson said, peeking around the corner from the hallway.

''You didn't walk on my clean floor, did you?'' Emma asked.

''No, I floated in,'' Wes said, striding into the room, a wide grin on his face.

Christie rose and kissed her father's cheek. ''How are you, Daddy?''

''Good. And you?'' He gazed at her with knowing eyes. ''I suppose you know—'' He looked from Emma back to Christie.

Christie squeezed his arm and settled back into her chair. ''I knew before I came here. No problem. I'll live with it.''

''I know you will,'' he said, leaning his shoulder against the doorframe. ''And anyway, you have Milton now.''

''But I'm not sure, Dad. Milton's looking toward marriage, and I'm not.''

Wes scratched his head as if he didn't understand. "You have to be honest with him, Christie."

"I am honest, Dad. I—"

Her father leaned closer. "If he's pushing you toward marriage, and you feel it's wrong—"

"The Bible says it's wrong," Emma said, frowning at her husband.

"Well, not anymore." Wes pulled back and gave them both a decisive look.

"What do you mean?" Christie asked, puzzled by the statement.

"The way I look at it, Patrick has a son and that means he—h-he must have had relations to do it."

His discomfort made Christie uneasy. "But we were divorced then, Daddy. That doesn't count. It wasn't adultery."

"By jingo, Wes, you're right," Emma said. "I'd never thought of it like that." She swiveled toward Christie, her eyes filled with hope. "You see, Christie, in God's eyes it was. Now if you have feelings for Milton, then maybe—"

"That's not all of it, Mom." Frustration heated her face. "You're not listening to me. It's just—"

"Let the girl be, Emma," Wes said. "You and I need to butt out and let Christie make decisions for herself. She's old enough." He gave her a good-natured wink and headed out of the room. "Want a soda, Christie? Emma?" he asked from the hallway outside the kitchen.

"No thanks, Dad. I need to get going soon."

Emma shook her head.

"Then I'll just float in and get one for myself." He gave Emma a bigger grin and vanished through the doorway.

Christie heard him in the kitchen, banging around as loudly as her riled mood. She'd known it was coming so why let it bother her? It's natural for parents to want to shield their children from hurt. She'd do the same if she had a child.

Christie rose and pulled her bag from the chair near the entry. "I need to go, Mom."

Emma rose, her face puckered with disappointment. "Will we see you in church Sunday?"

"I don't know, Mom." She watched greater sadness fill her mother's eyes. "I'll see. Maybe."

The "maybe" did it. Her mother smiled and patted her arm as if *maybe* meant *for sure.*

Christie walked across the church parking lot. Sometimes she wondered if Jemma and her mother were in cahoots about her church attendance. She trudged up the stairs into the building and stood in the sanctuary doorway, searching for Jemma.

Spotting her and Philip near the front, Christie moved down the aisle and slid into the pew beside Jemma. Philip gave her a nod.

"You made it," Jemma said, pleasure spreading over her face.

"How could I resist when you said Ellie wanted me here?"

Jemma chuckled and patted Ellie's head leaning against her arm. "Claire came, too." She motioned to her former mother-in-law beside Philip.

Christie leaned across her friend and nodded to Claire, then acknowledged Ellie squeezed between her mom and dad. "I heard you're going to sing with the nursery class today."

Ellie nodded. "'Jesus Loves Me.' Her piping voice sounded above the hum of parishioners.

"I like that song," Christie said, giving her cheek a pat and settling back against the bench. "Have you talked with my mother?" she asked Jemma.

"Your mother? No. Why?"

"She's been bugging me about coming to church, then you called and asked me to come, too." Christie gave Jemma a playful arch of her eyebrow.

"I'm innocent." She lifted her hands and made a little cross over her heart with her index finger.

Thinking of her parents, Christie swivelled and looked over her shoulder to see where they were. They always sat in the same church pew. She spotted them and sent them a smile, but before she turned back, her lungs froze as she looked into Patrick's eyes. Patrick in church? He never attended worship.

She yanked her head around and riveted her attention to the altar, but a strong desire rose to look back again. She'd noticed Sean nestled beside Patrick and his father. Years had passed since she'd talked with Mr. Hanuman.

The child's presence poked at her awareness. Patrick's child with another woman. Could she ever forget that? Could she ever forgive that? Still the absurd paradox, the child's guiltless face tugged at her heart. Children—so innocent and so hopeful. If only those attributes lasted. But life soon marched in to destroy innocence and smother hope.

What if things had been different?

The thought shifted to questions. What was Patrick doing in church? He'd been a staunch non-attender. If he believed, he'd never let on, and Christie always assumed it wasn't as important to him as it was to her.

Seeing Patrick's father in church, too, made her wonder. He'd never been a churchgoer either. Perhaps, as her mother had said, old age and fear of dying had brought Joe Hanuman to seek the Lord. He had a heart condition Patrick had said. Christie felt a deep shame and lifted her eyes to the cross. Who was she to question why he was in church or judge anyone's heart? She didn't even know her own.

Music for the first hymn sounded. She rose with the congregation, singing the familiar tune. After the pastor's greeting and prayer, the nursery-school children paraded forward—some coaxed and some advancing with the confidence of Pavarotti. They lined up like stair steps and sang the familiar song with sweet, angelic voices. Christie's heart lifted with the music then fell with the knowledge she would never hear her own child sing the simple, faith-filled song.

When the children returned to their seats amidst the grins of proud parents and friends, the pastor spoke and lessons were read while Christie's mind drifted, but within the murmur of the scripture reading, words struck her awake. *And when you stand praying, if you hold anything against anyone, forgive him, so that your Father in heaven may forgive you your sins.*

Christie looked up to see where the words had come from. Foolish. She eyed the lay reader. For a moment, she thought the words she'd heard had come directly from God. The message had jolted her like a lightning bolt. Forgiveness? She wanted to forgive Patrick with every beat of her heart, but *want* and *could* were two separate concepts. No question, she wanted the Lord's forgiveness, but if she had to forgive Patrick first, she might never receive God's mercy.

Christie hoped the Lord could see her situation was different. Patrick had walked out on her, not the other way around. He was the one who needed to ask for forgiveness.

The rest of the service was lost in her rumination until the organ's diapason roused her to stand and join in the final hymn.

As the congregation filed down the aisle, Christie lifted Ellie in her arms and gave her a kiss on the cheek. "You were wonderful," she said to the child who nodded her head in full agreement.

Claire swooped in to give Christie a hug. Her bracelets jangled and the ruffled crinkle-crepe top—right out of the seventies—seemed too youthful for her years, but that was Claire. Her heart was as spirited as her wardrobe.

When Claire released her, Jemma touched Christie's arm. "Before I lose you, how about going with me to the Chamber of Commerce Fourth of July family picnic? I realize you don't usually go, but I assume Loving Care will be closed that day."

Without a family, Christie didn't often attend. "We're closed, but what about Philip? And don't you usually have an employee party that day?"

"Usually, but Philip will be out of town this year. I want to go to the Chamber event, but I'd rather have company."

Christie regarded Jemma's pleading look and figured she would enjoy getting out with her good friend alone for a change. "Sure. Next Friday?"

"Right. You'll go?"

"Sounds fine," she said, feeling another hand nudge her shoulder. She turned to see her mother and father behind her. Her mother's face glowed with delight.

"Mark this date on your calendar," Christie said, pecking each parent's cheek. "I'm here like you asked.

"We noticed," Emma said.

"I promised Jemma I'd come to hear Ellie sing."

Emma's smile faded. "Doesn't matter what reason."

Christie kicked herself. "And my mom asked me to come, too." She sent her mother a reassuring smile, wishing she'd be more thoughtful with her comments.

"We're glad you're here," her father said.

"Thanks, Daddy. Me, too."

As they headed off, Patrick gave her an amiable wave and she stood still, not wanting to deal with any more issues today. She hadn't spoken to his father since she and Patrick had separated so long ago, but today she felt a pang for the man. His illness had taken a deep toll on his appearance. His pale, drawn face barely resembled the ruddy man from her past. Avoiding him made no sense. It was like her not attending worship: it made her feel sorrowful and guilty.

Guilty? Why would she feel guilty? The divorce had been Patrick's desire, not hers.

As she left her thoughts, Patrick appeared beside her. Christie looked across the room and saw Sean with his grandfather.

"Hello, Patrick."

"I wondered if I'd see you here," he said.

His statement unsettled her. "I don't attend as much as I used to. Haven't for a while." Eight years, she added to her thoughts.

"You never missed church. I remember that," he said.

"Like everything else, that was long ago."

"Dad's here." He tilted his head in his father's direction.

"I noticed."

Silence surrounded them, and Christie knew she had to say more.

"He doesn't look like himself. I'm sorry."

Patrick shrugged. "Time and age. It comes to us all."

The comment hit her like a hammer. One day a wrinkled body and old age would be hers.

"Unless we die before our time," he added.

His unsettling comment threw her off-kilter. His wife had died before her time. It could happen to anyone. Any time. A knot caught in her throat, and she could only nod.

He stood beside her a moment, a look of apprehension on his face as if he had something more to say and was afraid to say it.

Christie didn't make things easier. If she acted on her heart, she would touch his face and smooth away the stress, but she acted with her head. She did nothing.

He shifted his feet and dug his hands into his pockets. "Dad's waiting for me." He tilted his head toward his father.

She nodded and turned away before he saw the tears that sprang to her eyes.

* * *

Patrick rose from the picnic bench. "How about a drink, Dad. A soda or some coffee?"

"Decaf if they have it," Joe said, turning back to speak with an old Chamber of Commerce crony.

"Keep an eye on Sean."

His father nodded, and Patrick turned away and headed for the refreshments. As he neared the area, he faltered. Christie stood across an expanse of grass beside Jemma Somerville. He hadn't expected Christie at the Chamber of Commerce picnic, but why not? She owned a local business.

He took a step toward her, then halted. Should he or shouldn't he? The last time he'd tried to be amiable, Christie had seemed uneasy. That's the last way he wanted to make her feel.

Instead of approaching her, he poured the coffee, picked up his soft drink, then returned to his father.

From the corner of his eye, he watched Christie move among the members, stopping to visit, her face unstressed, her smile sincere. Patrick wished they could return to that comfortable friendship they'd had once. She had been a good wife until his own fears had waylaid their marriage. Then she'd turned cold and aloof.

He knew Christie strove for excellence. She wanted things done well or not at all. Their marriage had failed. Her perfect world had ripped and fluttered to the ground like a balloon scraped through gnarled tree limbs. Patrick had let her down.

Forcing his thoughts aside, he smiled at Sean who was watching him from beside his grandfather. Patrick slid the paper coffee cup onto the table. "Here you go, Dad."

His father nodded, returning to his conversation, while Patrick popped the top of the soda and took a swig. His gaze shifted back to Christie before he searched in his small cooler for Sean's milk and plastic cup.

Handing his son the drink, Patrick felt a hand on his shoulder. Christie? His heart dipped and rose before he turned.

"Patrick, when did you get back in town?"

His eyes and ears struggled to accept reality. "Jason Briggs, how in the world are you?" Patrick stuck out his hand, pleased to see his old high-school friend.

"Couldn't be better. I own Briggs Commercial Design over on Capital. Drop by some time, and I'll show you around." He released Patrick's hand. "So what brings you back home?"

Patrick motioned to his father. "Dad's been ill, and I'm back to run the hardware."

Jason's smile faded when he looked at Joe Hanuman. "Sorry. Wish you were coming home on better terms."

"It's life," Patrick said, shrugging.

"Did you notice Christie's here? I saw her across the way." Jason gestured with his elbow.

Did he notice? That's all he could think about.

"We've talked since I've been back." Wondering how long it had been since he'd spoken with Jason, Patrick motioned toward Sean. "This is my son."

Jason smiled at the boy, then eyed the others at the table with a puzzled look.

Patrick answered his unspoken question. "My wife died a couple of years ago so I'm doing my best."

"Whoa, man. You've had your hands full." Jason grasped Patrick's shoulder and gave it a shake. "Sorry to hear that. I heard you'd married again." He studied Sean a moment, then tilted his head toward Christie. "She's never remarried, you know. Any hope of—"

"None at all." The unfinished question whirred in Patrick's head. If only… He let the words fade. If only nothing. Christie's feeble attempts to be civil had underscored his response. Congeniality, even friendship were doubtful at this point.

His brisk response seemed to knock the wind out of Jason. He'd been an usher at their wedding, and Patrick wished he'd been more subtle. Jason had known Christie and him when they were young and happy.

Jason's look eased, and he grasped Patrick's forearm. "Listen. Let's get together one of these days. My sister could use some cheering up. She's been divorced a couple of years and not doing much. Maybe we could go out together sometime. You know, just for fun."

Patrick nodded, but his spirit slammed closed like a vault. He didn't want anyone trying to match him up with a woman, even a nice one like Jason's sister.

Not wanting to snub Jason, Patrick shrugged. "It's a possibility." He thought the answer left the door open for a rejection later.

"We'll talk later then," Jason said, his expression looking hopeful. "I'll call you."

"Sure," Patrick said. "Great seeing you."

Jason gave a farewell salute and turned away, leaving Patrick with a sense of doom. He slid onto the bench and shifted so he could see Christie. For a moment, she stood alone, sipping from a paper cup. Jason's unfinished question rang in his head. *Any hope of you and Christie getting back together?* Patrick's pulse tripped.

Fighting the unexpected emotion, he turned to check on Sean. He was kneeling on the bench, driving his toy trucks along the picnic table beside his grandfather. Patrick's heart swelled each time he looked at his son. The boy was all he needed. He'd tried marriage twice. It wasn't meant to be.

When he turned back and looked across the expanse of lawn, his gaze met Christie's and his heart stood still.

Chapter Five

Christie looked across the grass, riveted to Patrick's gaze. The picnic lunch she'd eaten churned in her stomach. She turned her eyes away from him and spotted Sean, then Joe Hanuman. What was he doing here when he was supposedly ill?

She should feel pleased the older man was well enough to attend the picnic just as he'd made it to church. Why did she dislike him so? The answer was clear. She disliked the situation—the constant reminder that he was her *ex*-father-in-law.

The *ex* was the culprit. Christie didn't want to be the ex of anything. She had wanted a storybook love—a romance like a sleeping princess kissed by the prince. She would have settled for a frog's kiss if it had turned into a prince. Anything but a failed marriage and divorce.

Divorce not only destroyed her perfect life, it took away all hope of having children—a longing that wove through her heart and plagued her dreams.

Christie steadied herself and searched through the milling crowd for Jemma. She saw her in deep conversation with another woman. Not wanting to interrupt, she let her gaze travel, looking for some place to go.

She eyed a group of younger children gathering across the way. Intrigued, Christie noticed Ellie among them. She turned toward Sean in time to see a woman guiding him to the other little ones. A game, she assumed and smiled as the boy marched toward the group without trepidation.

Taking a step to move closer to the activity, Christie faltered when a hand touched her arm. Without looking, she knew it was Patrick. She stopped and turned. "So, we meet again."

"My dad's getting a lifetime achievement award today. I'm his chauffeur."

"Lifetime achievement? That's really nice." She glanced toward the shriveled man who'd once been the picture of health. "Tell him I said congratulations."

"You could tell him yourself."

"No, I—I'd…Patrick, please don't push."

He drew back and studied her. "I'm the one who left you, Christie, not my dad."

His words startled her. She'd told herself the same

thing over and over so why did she continue to feel the way she did? "It's me, not your dad."

He allowed her apology to pass without comment. Instead, he breathed a sigh. "Sean's occupied for a while."

"I noticed. Nice they have games for the kids."

He nodded, though his eyes seemed unfocused and distracted.

"Christie, could we talk?" he asked. "Just for a few minutes? I told Dad I was going for a walk. Will you come with me? It won't take long?"

His expression pleaded, and her heart softened. What good was refusal? If they talked, he'd get off his chest whatever he still wanted to say and leave her be. Leave her be? Strangely, the idea left her lonely.

"Okay. For a few minutes, but I'm not sure this is the place. I'd hate for gossip—"

"It's been a long time, Christie. Most of these people don't even realize we know each other."

The truth of his words made her smile. "I suppose you're right."

She moved into step with him, and they followed the park's path toward the old lighthouse. A summer breeze blew off Lake Michigan, and through the trees, Christie could see the sun sprinkle the lake with fairy dust. A perfect day.

Feeling Patrick beside her, a sense of déjà vu permeated her. She and Patrick had walked this same path years earlier when they'd come back to Loving for visits with their folks. She loved the peace and the feel of history lingering around the old Loving Light. Her hair ruffled in the wind, and she brushed it back, drawing in the scent of sun and lake.

Farther along, Patrick headed for a bench spattered with sunlight and shade. She followed, and they settled on the rough boards facing the water, neither speaking. She clung to the silence, enjoying the July heat and a strange inward warmth. Resolve. Perhaps they would settle the inner turmoil and get on with their lives.

She sidled a look at Patrick, his strong classic profile and dark hair creating a deep ache within her. Times had been so good back then. Christie bit back the desire to ask him why he was so quiet when he'd come here to talk.

"Don't be angry if I tell you how nice it is to sit beside you again," Patrick said, out of the blue.

The sound of his voice jolted the silence. She wanted to tell him she felt the same, but she swallowed the words. "It's a lovely day" was all she said.

He shifted toward her, his face thoughtful. "Life hasn't been easy for either of us. I know it hasn't been for me."

Christie wanted to tell him how difficult it had been. Instead, she shrugged.

"I just want to tell you how sorry I am about everything. I'm sorry I messed up your life. I didn't know how to make a successful marriage. I'm not sure I even knew what to expect from one.'' He shifted, resting his elbows on his knees, his eyes facing the ground. ''My folks' marriage was no example for me, as you know.''

To her surprise, he moved toward her and touched her arm. ''I'm not making excuses, Christie. I'm just sorry I didn't realize what a mess I was.''

Though emotion twisted through her, Christie clung to her defenses. She'd refused to allow herself to be hurt again by any man, but his confession left her wondering. ''So what made the difference?''

He looked at her as if he didn't understand.

''I mean why did you try again? What made you think marriage would work a second time?''

Emotion charged across his face—a blend of expressions that left Christie uncertain how he felt.

He drew in a lengthy breath. ''I found the Lord. That's what made the difference.''

His answer stunned her. He'd found the Lord and she'd lost a piece of her faith. *God works in mysterious ways.* ''I spoke with you at church, but I figured you were there for your father.''

''For both of us. I know it's difficult to imagine. While I was gone, Dad recognized the emptiness in his life and realized it wasn't from without but from within. I learned the same lesson.''

Emptiness within. Resentment poked at her. Why did he have to say that? She'd felt empty too, since he'd been gone—the kind of emptiness that didn't go away.

Patrick's face brightened and his voice sparked with enthusiasm. "I had always seen peace and joy in your life, Christie, and never understood it. I resented it because I felt cheated. I'd never known that comfort. Not only did you have God, but you had a mother and father. A completed family. I had none of that."

"You knew that when you married me."

"I know, but I didn't understand it…me. I didn't understand me and how all that affected my life until it was too late."

Too late. The words had a double ring to them now. It was too late then, and it was too late now. She blanketed the longing that pushed against her heart. "I'm sorry it happened, too, Patrick. At least we've each gotten on with our lives." An unexpected empathy rattled her. "I know it's hard for you now, alone with Sean, but you're a good father and you're still a family. You have each other."

"Yes. I have Sean," he said. "That's what's kept me going. I'm glad you have the child-care center. I know it's different, but you love kids so…" His voice faded as if he didn't know where to go with his comment.

"It's not family, but I enjoy it," she said, not wanting him to pity her.

He glanced at his watch and rose. "I suppose we'd better get back. They'll be doing the award soon, and I can't leave my dad with Sean too long."

She stood and followed him back down the path.

"I'd still like to see your place sometime if you'd let me. Loving Care, I mean. I'm really proud of you."

How many times had he asked? How many times had she pushed him away? For what? "Sure, Patrick. Drop by whenever. I'm always there."

"Thanks," he said.

His sincere words and smile rolled before her like rose petals along the path, making her feel admired and special.

But reality struck her, and the rose-petal path faded as her defensive wall rose.

She didn't want to feel drawn to Patrick.

Patrick slipped his knit shirt over his head and gazed at himself in the mirror. He'd aged, noticeably, in the years since Sherry had died. Leaning closer, he noticed a couple of white hairs glinting among the black near his temple. He felt tempted to use tweezers to pluck out the telltale signs of aging, but he was pushing forty—two and a half years from it—and a few strands of gray would add a little sophistication to his character.

He blew a stream of air from his lungs and dropped the comb into the dresser drawer. Why he'd agreed to the invitation for dinner with Jason and his wife was beyond him. No doubt they'd want to know about his second marriage, and he felt certain Christie would come into the conversation. But they'd been longtime friends. How could he refuse?

The bonus was they'd invited him to bring Sean since they had a boy about the same age. The kids would add a measure of distraction to the evening and give him a good excuse to go home early.

Patrick slipped on his sport jacket, took one more look in the mirror, then headed downstairs. Sean waited for him at the bottom, looking spiffed up with the help of Grandpa. "Lookin' good, Sean," he said, descending the last three steps. "Grandpa did a good job."

His father stood in the living-room doorway, his shoulder resting against the jamb. "You two make a handsome couple."

"Thanks, Dad, and thanks for the finishing touches on Sean."

"My pleasure. Now go and have a nice time. Tell Jason and his wife I said hello."

"I'll do that," he said, opening the door. His father had always liked Jason. He had been Patrick's boyhood friend. They'd watched each other mature, succeed and fail in school, fall in love and get married. But Jason's marriage had lasted. His hadn't.

Sean meandered outside, and Patrick followed. With a solid hook on the car seat belt, they were on their way. In minutes, he pulled in front of a white bungalow with black shutters, brightened by colorful beds of flowers. The word *cozy* came to mind.

Patrick unlatched Sean from the seat, and they headed up the walk. Jason met them at the door, sending nostalgic feelings creeping into Patrick's thoughts.

"Glad you could come," Jason said, holding the door open.

"Thanks for inviting us." Patrick knew it was a half truth, but he decided his comment was one of those acceptable social phrases that didn't mean much anyway.

Sean was met at the living-room doorway by Jason's toddler, Brent. The boys shied away for a heartbeat, then gave in to curiosity.

When Patrick swung through the arch, expecting to see Jason's wife, Diane, he stopped in his tracks. "Roseann. How are you?" He cringed inwardly, realizing that Jason had decided to play matchmaker without giving Patrick an option.

"Good, and you?"

"Well, getting adjusted to Loving. I didn't have much time after the move before I had to take over the hardware."

She stood beside her chair, looking uneasy. "I'm sure it's been hard, especially with…" She tilted her head toward Sean.

"Sean," Patrick said, wondering where Jason and Diane had vanished to.

"Yes. Sean."

He stood there, unable to sit while she was standing.

"Have a seat, Patrick," she finally said, giving a

broad gesture toward the chairs and ending at the space beside her on the sofa.

Asking himself again why he'd accepted Jason's invitation, Patrick selected a chair and settled into it, his hands folded in his lap. He should have known his friend wanted to hook him up with Roseann. Jason had mentioned it at the picnic. The problem wasn't Roseann. Patrick lifted his gaze to her pretty face. She was a nice woman. He just wasn't ready to get involved with anyone right now, especially since Christie…

Sounds at the doorway gave him reprieve, and he focused there, waiting for someone to enter. Diane came through the archway, looking pleased to see him.

"I'm so glad Jason spotted you at the picnic. I'm happy you could come. It's been a long time."

"It has. Thanks for having me," he said, feeling the evening going nowhere.

"It'll be fun," she said, glancing toward Roseann and then excusing herself again.

Jason passed her in the doorway and wandered in, chewing on something from the kitchen, then plopped into a chair. "So, how's it going?"

"Okay. I have lots to get settled yet, but I'm getting into the groove."

"You're taking over your dad's business, you said."

Patrick nodded. "Right."

Jason tilted his head toward the kids playing on the floor. "What are you doing about Sean?"

The question unsettled Patrick's thoughts. He'd treated the dilemma with bandages, trying to patch solutions that only masked the issue. "That's still a bit of a problem. Dad's been feeling pretty good so he keeps an eye on him for a while during the day. I come home for lunch, but I really need to find a sitter. Know anyone?"

"Diane might have a name or two. We have a couple of girls who sit with Brent and Jill." He ran his fingers through his hair. "Jill's spending the night with a girlfriend. She's ten."

Patrick nodded, knowing he should be saying something interesting, but his brain cells had shriveled since he'd walked into the house and seen Roseann.

"How about Christie's place? She has a day care."

"Right, but I'm a little hesitant about asking her."

"Hey, it's business. She wants your money. You want a sitter. Makes sense."

Diane's call from the doorway sent Jason back to the kitchen. She gave him a grin. "We'll be ready to eat in a minute. I hope you're hungry."

"Sure am, and I'm tired of eating my own cooking," Patrick said.

Diane vanished into the kitchen, and seeing the

glow on Roseann's face made him want to eat his words.

"I know," Roseann said. "It's so difficult to cook for one person, except you have Sean."

"And my father," Patrick said.

"That's right." A faint flush rose from under her collar.

She shifted in the chair, looking about as comfortable as a cat in a dog house, and he did nothing to ease her tension. Hoping Diane or Jason would return to add something to the conversation, Patrick glanced toward the door but no one appeared.

"You heard I'm divorced," Roseann said, fiddling with the arm cover on the sofa.

"Jason mentioned it. I'm sorry."

"Going on two years." She glanced toward the children on the carpet, playing with building blocks. "I didn't have any children. I'm not sure if that's a blessing or not."

"It's a blessing," Patrick said. Noticing the expression on her face, he was sure that the comment didn't come off as he'd meant it. "I mean it's difficult raising a child alone."

"Yes, I'm sure it is. Your dad raised you alone, right?"

He felt a kick in the gut. Not that she meant it that way, but the comment sent shards of pain through him like broken glass. "Yes. That's right."

"He did a good job," she said, sending him a sweet smile.

Did he? Patrick wondered. His father had tried, but had he succeeded? Patrick thanked Roseann, wishing he could wiggle his nose and vanish. On the other hand, why couldn't he just treat Roseann like an old friend and not feel as if he'd been maneuvered into a matchmaking plot?

He listened while Roseann chattered about her life and asked him questions he begrudgingly answered. Finally, the room weighed heavy with silence, and Patrick's mind drifted back to the Chamber of Commerce picnic and his walk with Christie. For once, she'd been receptive to talk, and though an occasional edge had come into her voice, she'd been receptive. It gave him hope.

Hope? Hope for what? The word spun through his mind. Hope for friendship. Hope for healing. Hope for forgiveness. He'd take any one of them to start.

Christie's image that afternoon filled his mind. The sun had shone through the trees, blinking shadow and light on her honey-brown hair. Though at least five foot six, she seemed so small beside him. Small in size, but not in strength. Christie was strong. He'd realized that when he thought how successful she'd been…without him. She'd made her dream come true.

He could only fantasize that one day—

"Hungry?"

Diane's voice pierced his thoughts, and he refocused. "You bet."

"Okay. Come and get it."

He rose and caught a glimpse of disappointment in Roseann's face.

Chapter Six

Standing near the Lake Michigan shoreline, Christie stared across the water, wishing she'd not accepted Milton's invitation to the Loving Cup race. At the same time, she asked herself, why not? She couldn't find a better companion. He'd lavished her with attention and wonderful surprises—gifts, flowers and unexpected kindness.

Yet he'd made her uncomfortable so many times in the past months talking marriage while she'd avoided the topic. She'd used religion as an excuse. But was it that or her own fear? Her parents' comments filled her mind. Did God really consider Patrick's marriage adultery? Perhaps.

The question caused her to wonder about Milton. Maybe their relationship didn't ring bells and weaken her knees, but it was steady and secure. He knew she might never have children, and he'd said she was enough to make him happy.

Feeling his arm tighten around her shoulders, Christie looked into Milton's pleasant face, wishing she enjoyed the feelings that he'd expressed.

"Here they come," Milton said, using his free arm to point at the speck just breaking the horizon.

Christie focused on the small dot that grew closer as she watched. A small triangle of white, then another rose from the horizon, sailboats leaving Loving and racing to Holland, Michigan. She'd never seen the race before and was surprised to see the huge crowd that gathered along the lake's edge to watch.

"Pretty," she said, as the first vessel grew nearer, its scarlet hull cutting through the water.

He drew her closer and gazed into her eyes. "But not as pretty as you," he said.

Instead of her spirit leaping with his words, it sank like a barbell. Christie searched his face, wondering what was wrong with her. Was it fear of commitment? Fear of failure? Fear of love? Or was it the lack of love? The question bounced through her with the speed of the race they were watching.

"Thank you," she whispered, letting her gaze drift back to the sailboats surging past on sunlit waves. Her mind scurried to change the subject, to move to any topic other than their relationship.

"Look at the crowd," she said, pivoting toward the array of people spread out along the shoreline.

As her focus grazed the viewers, her breath caught short. She felt her shoulders droop and rise again as she swallowed her gasp.

Milton eyed her with curiosity, and with casual interest, he swiveled his head in the direction she'd looked. He didn't comment, and she couldn't. Patrick stood yards away. A woman stood beside him, smiling into his face, talking with animation, looking relaxed and enthralled at his attention.

In self-defense, Christie nestled closer to Milton. Why did it bother her to see Patrick with a woman? Why did she care what he did? They'd been divorced for years. He'd married, had a child, and now had another woman on his arm. What was new?

Nothing for Christie. She'd languished in self-pity, using her hurt and disappointment to drive her forward with her business. She'd allowed her faith issues to muddy her thoughts on marriage. Milton had asked her more than once, and he'd stuck by her even as she refused. Time had come to give him an answer. Either yes or no. She had to decide. Patrick had carved a new life for himself. Why shouldn't she?

Christie yanked open the door and stepped into the hardware store. She felt in her pocket for the list she'd prepared as she headed down the aisle. Walking past two clerks, she knew she should stop and ask where to find Peg-Board, but she hesitated. Her feelings swayed like a pendulum. One minute she avoided Patrick. The next minute, she manipulated situations to see him. Today, she longed to see him.

She looked at the note in her hand, realizing she'd crumpled it in her brooding. Patrick. He sat in her thoughts like an old sofa—comfortable and familiar, yet needing to be replaced with something new. She'd wrestled with indecision. Milton had asked her again about making a commitment—about marriage—when they went to dinner after the Loving Cup race. Instead of a firm "I'm not ready," Christie had given him hope. She'd promised him an answer...soon.

"Can I help you?"

Christie spun around at the question and peered at the young man. Disappointment washed over her, looking at the unfamiliar face. "Yes," she said, gaining her wits. "I'm looking for Peg-Board and brackets to mount it."

"Peg-Board?" A frown settled on his face while he raised a finger. "Just a minute." He turned and vanished around a display.

In a moment, she heard the young man's footsteps from the opposite direction. She turned. Instead, it was Patrick who looked at her, his face appearing as surprised as she felt.

"Peg-Board?" he asked, a grin rising to his lips. The cleft in his chin winked at her, sending her pulse skittering.

She nodded.

"What size?"

She shrugged and moved her arms to indicate the height and width she had in mind. With her arms spread like an eagle, she longed to wrap them around his neck, to feel the closeness of his body to hers, as she'd once done.

He beckoned her to follow, and she drew in a breath, holding back her emotion and locating the biting words that had been hers since she'd seen him at the races. She found them, but let them hang in her thoughts waiting to shoot them forward. *Who was that lady I saw you with?* Surprising herself, a grin tugged at her face when remembered the response to an old joke. *That was no lady. That was my wife.*

"You look cheerful today," Patrick said, sending her a warm smile as they stopped beside a gray double door. "Peg-Board that size is in the stock room. Come take a look."

He pushed open one of the doors, but she hesitated.

"Should I? What about—"

"The owner?" He chuckled. "He won't mind, I can assure you."

Realizing her foolishness, she stepped inside, and they sorted through the Peg-Boards until she found two that would fit the size she wanted at Loving Care. "I need mountings, too."

He hoisted the boards and tilted his head toward the door. "Can you get that?"

She held it open while he lugged the pieces

through, then set them on the floor and leaned them against the wall. Patrick led her to the brackets and located what she needed in the blink of an eye.

Christie grasped the hardware, longing to mention she'd seen him, but wondering how to bring it up without sounding catty. "Thanks for your help. You expedited the process."

"You're welcome." He glanced at his watch. "I'll help you carry the stuff to your car."

"That's not necess—"

He lifted his hand to stop her. "Go ahead to checkout, and I'll bring the Peg-Board up front."

She did as he said, and in moments, Patrick followed her outside, lugging her purchase. The boards didn't quite fit in her trunk, but Patrick had brought along a piece of twine and tied the trunk lid closed before she had time to wonder what to do.

"It's break time." He tilted his head toward a nearby coffee shop. "How about joining me for a cup of coffee?"

Her heart skipped, and she warned herself to be careful. Still, a few more minutes might give her the opportunity to learn something about the woman. The image of her smiling up at Patrick knotted in Christie's chest. She looked at her watch. "Maybe for a minute."

"Hold up, and I'll tell them I'll be back in fifteen." He bounded inside the store and out again in a second.

She felt him grasp her arm as he stepped beside

her, the feeling so familiar it sent longing stirring through her limbs. She wanted to pull away, but her reasoning lost the battle as they strode along the sidewalk. He let go when they reached the café, and paused to open the door. Inside, they sat at a table near the window. Christie ordered a latte while he asked for black coffee and cherry pie with ice cream. She'd forgotten how much he liked cherry pie.

When the waitress had come and gone, Christie settled into uneasy silence, wanting to broach the subject. ''How's your dad?'' she asked, hoping to segue somehow into her other question.

''Not good. I'm beginning to feel stressed out between Dad and Sean. With Dad so ill, I have another problem. Sean. I finally found a sitter. Diane Briggs gave me her name. You remember Di—''

Christie nodded, remembering her well. Jason had stood up at their wedding.

''The girl will sit with Sean during the day, at least, until school starts. Then I'll have to do something else.''

His eyes searched hers, and she realized what he was asking, but she wasn't ready to agree. How could she spend every day taking care of Patrick's child—a child that could have been hers if he'd been willing to try—back when her disease was new and she'd had a little hope. If only he'd listened to reason. But not Patrick. He knew…

She let the thought fade. In God's good time, her mother always said. Everything happened in God's time. So often she wondered why it couldn't be in her good time once in a while.

The waitress reappeared with their order, and Patrick delved into the cherry pie à la mode. Christie's stomach rumbled soundlessly, and she wished she'd ordered something. She took a sip of the frothy latte, enjoying the creamy taste.

"I saw you at the Loving Cup." The words shot from her mouth like a dart and cut through the silence.

Patrick lifted his head. "You did? Why didn't you say hi?"

Christie felt her jaw drop, and she slammed her mouth closed. "You had someone with you. I didn't want to interrupt."

"It was June. You remember her?"

"June?" Her memory slid to their high-school years, searching for the name, the face. "Not really."

"I suppose it's been a while. She lives in Long Branch now."

"Oh, that's nice." Stupid response, but her mind was tangled with June and why she should remember her.

"I still want to drop by your center, but with Dad sick and Sean, I haven't had time."

"I'm sorry things have been rough for you. Come anytime. No rush."

He studied her a moment, then dug into the dessert again and swallowed the last of his pie, washing it down with his coffee. "I'd better get back. Thanks for keeping me company."

"Thanks for carrying the Peg-Board to the car."

He grinned and rose.

The mundane conversation seemed so empty, so useless with all the thoughts that tumbled through her mind.

They stepped outside into the summer heat, and in a heartbeat, he'd vanished through the automatic door. She stood for a moment, clinging to the few minutes they'd spent together and feeling a sense of longing.

Longing? Who needed it? She hit the remote and yanked open her car door. The heat from inside overwhelmed her as did the emotion from within.

Patrick sank into the sofa. His feet were tired. His mind was tired. His spirit was tired. Before he had a chance to relax, Sean climbed onto his lap. "How's it goin', son?" He wrapped his arms around Sean's warm, wiggling body and gave him a kiss on the cheek. "Were you good for Tammy?"

"I was good," he said, tilting his head back and giving Patrick an open-mouthed smile.

"Nice teeth." He tousled his son's hair. "Did you remember to brush them today?"

Sean clamped his teeth together and jutted his chin forward for Patrick to take a look.

Patrick chuckled at his antics.

Sean slipped to the ground to drag out some toys,

and Patrick watched him, his mind filled with Christie's surprise appearance earlier in the day. He'd been trying to control his feelings. She looked so good to him when he saw her. Today she looked relaxed and comfortable with him. Her biting remarks were absent. She'd actually been friendly, even warm.

Warm. He'd asked himself the question before. Could he forget how cold and unloving she'd become before he left. *Bitter* seemed the word. But he'd not helped the situation, either. He'd closed her out, and she'd done the same. She probably didn't even know it.

But they'd both changed. She'd matured and had gained good business sense and confidence. He'd aged as well and now could see where they'd gone wrong. He wished they could start again. At least be friends, as they had been today.

"Finally home," Joe said, standing in the doorway. He clung to the doorjamb and stood a moment as if his feet couldn't move him forward.

"Not feeling well, Dad?"

"I'm okay. Just a little woozy."

Patrick jumped up and headed toward his father. "Let me help you to the chair."

His father shook his head. "I can walk. It just takes me a little time."

Frustrated, Patrick thought he had never known anyone as stubborn as his father. The thought gave him pause. Christie used to say the same about him. He couldn't imagine she was right.

"How are things working out with Tammy?" Patrick asked, following behind his father and trying to control the desire to escort him to the chair.

"She's a good girl," Joe said, slipping down into the recliner.

He made an effort to prop up the footrest and failed. Patrick leaned down and pulled up the lever, receiving an instant frown from his father. Patrick ignored it and returned to the sofa.

"I'm sorry I'm late, Dad. I just couldn't get out of the store today. I'm glad Tammy stayed on."

His father's interest piqued when he'd mentioned the store. Patrick took a moment to fill him in on the problem he'd run into with an order and to explain why they were short of help today.

"I suppose I should think about dinner," Patrick said, remembering years ago when he came home from work tired and Sherry had had a roast in the oven or a steak on the grill. Now they lived on frozen dinners, carryout and an occasional meal he actually cooked. He rose and took a step toward the kitchen.

"No problem," Joe said. "Tammy made a hamburger casserole." He swung his hand in the direction of the kitchen. "We left some in the refrigerator."

Patrick wandered toward the fridge and yanked open the door. A baking dish sat on the middle shelf, its edges crispy brown. He popped the conglomeration into the microwave and grabbed a plate from the cabinet. When the buzzer sounded, he opened the door and a pleasant scent enveloped him.

He'd only eaten a couple of forkfuls when his father appeared at the doorway and made his way to a wooden chair. The legs scraped on the linoleum as he dragged it away from the table and sat across from Patrick. "Not bad, eh?"

"Not bad at all." Patrick lifted another forkful of the meaty macaroni mixture.

"I've been thinking," Joe said.

Patrick lifted his eyes, feeling a frown settle on his forehead. "About what?"

"Christie."

"Christie?" His curiosity grew. "I ran into her today at the hardware store."

"You did?" He fiddled with the earpiece of his glasses. "She come to see you?"

"Buying Peg-Board. Anyway, what do you mean you've been thinking about her?"

"I don't know." His gaze wandered a moment while he thought. "She doesn't talk to me anymore, and I'd like to fix that."

"Fix it? How?"

"Make amends. I don't know. You're back, and it seems like we should be talking, too. You're the one she divorced. Not me."

Though Patrick felt a grin flash across his face, his dad was right. Christie did seem to avoid his father, and with his health. But what could he do? Christie was as stubborn as he was. That's one thing that hadn't changed. "I suppose I could mention you'd like to see her, Dad."

"That'd be nice." He motioned toward the casserole dish. "Any of that left?"

Patrick's spirit lifted. "Sure." He sprang to his feet and piled some of the food onto a plate. "You need to eat more, Dad. You don't eat enough."

"Enough for what?"

Enough for what? Patrick set the plate in front of his dad. "Just enough."

His father's question rang in his head. *Enough for what?* What was enough for Patrick? Not food, but life? He'd let so much slide. So much had faded in his life since he'd become an adult. Yes, he'd found his faith. That had been a revelation. Sean had filled his time and kept him going. But was that enough? Life seemed so long and terribly lonely without someone to share it with.

Chapter Seven

Christie stepped into the cooler shadows of the lovely old church and stood in the archway, searching for her mother's salt-and-pepper hair and the cute little bald spot on her father's head.

She spotted them and scurried down the aisle before the service began. When she slid into the pew, her mother's face made it all worthwhile. Her father leaned across to give her a nod before the organ hit the resounding chord for the first hymn.

The congregation rose, and Christie followed, lifting the thick songbook in her hands, flipping with her finger until she found the page. "Majesty." The words soared to the vaulted ceiling and reverberated against the thick wooden beams.

She loved the old building. Though modern churches with auditorium seating were popular, her fidelity clung to the tried and true—the church in the wildwood as the old hymn rendered.

As the praise song surrounded her, she thought about the past weeks. She knew she was headed for trouble with Patrick back in her life. More hurt. More sadness. And when Sean came to mind, envy knifed through her, and the whole horrible situation settled over her again. Would it ever go away?

When the song ended, Christie sat and slid the book into the rack as she watched the pastor rise for the welcome and announcements. Her mind drifted to the last time she'd seen Patrick. The name *June* had dangled in her head the past days, and Christie tried to recall who she was. Patrick had seemed so certain she should know the woman. But she couldn't put a face to the name. Curious, Christie swiveled her head and spotted Patrick and Sean. Her heart sank when she noticed the same woman beside him. June.

Having no time to study the woman's face, hoping for recognition, Christie turned back when she heard the pastor announce a reading from Luke 6. She opened the pew Bible, flipped through the pages until she found the lesson and followed along. Her stomach twisted with the vision of Patrick and June together behind her, until a passage stopped her cold. *Do not judge, and you will not be judged. Do not condemn, and you will not be condemned. Forgive, and you will be forgiven.*

She sensed the lesson was for her. It had shot

through the air and landed against her heart, but what had she judged? Who had she condemned? She had been entangled in envy. She knew that was a sin.

The evidence seemed clear. Patrick and the woman. She'd seen them together twice and had made a judgment about them. She had no right to be jealous. Her mind whirred with puzzling thoughts. Why had he invited Christie for coffee if he had a relationship with June? Why did he persist in wanting to visit Loving Care? Why was he riling her emotions when he had another woman at his side?

She felt deceived again. He'd walked out on her once before, and today she felt as if he'd knocked on her door and then slammed it shut when she'd answered. *Forgive, and you will be forgiven.*

The words nudged her, and she closed her eyes, asking God to help her understand the anguish she felt. Why? Why did Patrick come back to town and confuse her life? She would move—go somewhere else if she didn't have Loving Care. Loving care. That's what she needed now. *Lord, forgive me for my lax faith and keep me in Your loving care.*

She pushed her shoulders back against the pew and took a breath, feeling a calm settle over her. She had to trust God if no one else. Keeping her mind focused on the message and prayers, Christie rose for the final hymn, relieved. She prayed she could make a speedy escape and not have to deal with

Patrick, June or anyone. She'd find her sanctuary at home. Alone.

"Good to see you," her mother said to her as the service ended.

Christie spoke with them briefly, then made a quick excuse and turned to slip out the side door.

"Where you running off to?"

She stood still as Patrick's voice surrounded her. Trapped. Garnering courage, she turned to face him. The young woman stood at his side, her face pleasant and genial.

Christie felt her eyes shifting like a search light from one to the other, unable to speak.

"This is June," he said.

"Hi. We've met before." June stuck out her hand and Christie shook it, numbed with bewilderment.

June chuckled. "You don't remember. I was at your wedding."

Wedding? So long ago. How could Christie remember anything of that day? She had been so filled with excitement and wonder.

"I'm Patrick's cousin from Long Branch."

Cousin. Long Branch. Christie looked at June, dazed that she'd forgotten. She'd only met her once—at the wedding. "I'm sorry, June. The wedding was—"

"No need to apologize. I lived in California for a while after that so I wasn't around when you and Patrick were…" Her voice faded, and she gave Patrick a helpless look. "I'm sorry. I shouldn't—"

"No problem," Christie said. "I understand."

Relief swept across June's face as it had already whisked over Christie.

"I've been wanting to drive over to see Uncle Joe, but my schedule has been so crazy," June said. "I'm glad I came."

"That's great you could visit," Christie said, managing to cover her embarrassment.

Patrick rested his hand on June's shoulder. "She's been good for Dad. He's having so much fun talking about old times when June's dad and he were boys. Too bad she has to leave today."

June agreed, and Christie struggled to listen to the conversation while her mind filled with awe. She'd only asked God moments earlier for help and already He'd answered her prayer. *Do not judge, and you will not be judged.*

The words struck her. She'd judged and condemned. Yet God had answered her prayer in the blink of an eye. Another reality struck her. Jealousy. She'd envied June while concocting a romance between her and Patrick. The feeling startled her. Christie tuned back into the conversation, realizing that she needed so much more from the Lord. More than she could ever give in return.

Patrick stood near the stock room amazed at the traffic in the store. Fix-up time, he assumed. The weather had been perfect for outdoor repairs, so business was good.

His thoughts were with his father. He would miss June. Her visit had given him so much pleasure, and Patrick had noticed lately that his father's coloring had faded. He looked pale and drawn. Time to see the doctor, he figured. He checked his watch, anxious to have the day end.

As he turned, his stomach knotted. Jason's sister, Roseann, was heading his way, her smile as bright as a beacon. She waved, and Patrick lifted his hand in greeting.

"How are you?" she said, closing the distance.

"Busy today," he said, keeping the focus on business.

She pivoted and eyed the customers. "I suppose it keeps bread on the table." She searched his face.

Patrick recognized her discomfort but had no way to offer her assurance. She was a nice person, but his thoughts were in too many places to deal with romance.

"Jason thought you'd give him a call," she said. "He hasn't seen you around."

"I haven't been socializing much. My life's not my own lately."

"You have to have fun sometime," she said.

"Between my dad and Sean, I have my hands full." And then there was Christie. He wished her image didn't rise into every conversation.

"I realize that." She tucked her hands in her pants pockets and faltered. "I like kids a lot. I'd love to come over and make you a home-cooked dinner. Or even baby-sit, if you need me.''

Patrick's knotted stomach became a tourniquet. ''That's really kind, Roseann. Right now I have a sitter.''

''I'd hoped to see you or maybe get a phone call,'' she said.

Honesty, Patrick thought. Why beat around the bush? He could save the woman embarrassment by telling her the truth.

''You and Jason have been friends a long time, and so have we. I thought that—''

''I think I need to clear the air, Roseann. You're a very nice woman, and, you're right, we've been friends a long time. Right now, I'm struggling with some issues.'' He felt as miserable as Roseann, and he shuffled his feet looking for a way to be kind.

''I have someone else on my mind, and—''

''It's Christie, isn't it?''

He nodded.

''I thought so.''

''We were married seven years before I walked out on her. I'd like a chance to explore that relationship if she'll let me.''

''I'm here,'' Roseann said, ''if you need a friend.''

''Thanks,'' he said, extending his hand.

She placed her fingers in his, her hand clammy and limp. He could see discouragement in her eyes.

"Tell Jason I said hi," Patrick said. "I'll try to call him one of these days."

She stepped back and gave him a nod before turning away.

Patrick watched her go, realizing how rejection must feel. He'd turned his back on Christie, too. If he'd inherited one trait from his mother, it was avoidance.

"I'm so happy for you," Christie said, giving Annie a hug. "So when will you bring home the baby?"

"In another month. At twelve months she's not exactly a baby." Annie's face beamed. "Ken is ecstatic. He can't believe he's going to be a father."

"She couldn't have two more perfect parents," Christie said, poked by a smidgen of envy, but if the joy wasn't to be hers, she delighted in Annie and Ken's happiness.

"Thanks, Christie. For two old codgers, this will be such an experience."

"Old codgers? You're both in your forties."

"Right, but that's old to begin parenting." Annie's face brightened. "But God is on our side. I know we'll have to adjust, but it's what we want. We've prayed for this day."

"It's wonderful, Annie. I can't wait to meet her."

"You can be our first visitor." Annie gave her another hug and bounded from the room with more energy than Christie had seen in her since they'd met. Annie had been a good employee. Just the kind of person Christie had needed—motherly and loving and with a passel of wisdom.

Christie turned toward her desk and stopped at the work table, catching a glimpse of the blueprints for the addition. She needed to get things settled. She'd been so scattered she hadn't remembered to make the bank appointment. She moved to her desk and made a note to do that. While she was there, she added Milton to her note. She wanted to contact him when he returned from his business trip to give him her answer, an answer she should have given a long time ago.

As the thought left her mind, the telephone jingled. Christie lifted the receiver with a secret hope.

"Christie? Hi. I'm back."

Milton. Her heart dipped and rose to her throat. "How did it go?" She always asked and he would expect it.

"Wonderful, but I missed you."

She couldn't say it. It would be a lie. "Milton."

"Yes?" The enthusiasm had drained from his tone.

"We need to talk."

Christie backed out of the parking lot and rolled out onto the highway. She needed something to fortify her spirit. She'd agreed to have dinner with Milton on Friday. Tomorrow.

A yellow light flashed to red, and Christie pressed

her foot on the brake. Looking ahead, she saw the Dairy Dip. Ice cream. If anything fortified her and gave her courage, it would be something sweet and creamy on a hot day. The late-July temperature had been in the nineties.

When the light changed, she crossed the intersection and turned into the parking lot, rolling past a couple of outdoor umbrella tables. The image of a man with dark hair and classic profile flashed past her window as she pulled into a spot. She sat a moment, her eyes looking heavenward at the roof of her car. *Lord, is this your work?*

She stepped out and validated she'd been correct. Patrick and Sean sat at an umbrella table.

"Hi," she said, as she neared them.

"Christie," he said.

"This must be a day for an ice-cream cone."

"Ice-cweam cone," Sean repeated, holding up his treat for Christie to see.

She smiled at the boy as Patrick rose to greet her, and she grinned at him, seeing him so formal. She remembered times near the end of their marriage when she had walked into a room and he didn't acknowledge her presence.

"Have a seat." He motioned toward an empty chair. "What would you like?"

"I'll get it," she said, moving past.

He touched her arm. "Let it be my treat. Vanilla and chocolate swirl? You used to like those."

Touched by his remembering, she grinned. "I still do."

He gestured again to the seat beside him. "Keep an eye on Sean, and I'll be right back."

She slid into the chair and turned her attention to the boy. His cheeks were rosy from the sun, and she noticed his skin had tanned to a rich shade as Patrick's always did in the summer. Chocolate ice cream had smeared his mouth and ran from his chin.

"Does that taste good, Sean?" she asked.

He nodded his head, his tongue too busy catching drips.

Christie lifted a napkin from the table and wiped the goo before it fell to his knit shirt.

He looked down at the napkin, then back to her with a giggle.

"Here you go," Patrick said, slipping into the plastic chair and handing her the cone wrapped in a napkin.

"Thanks," she said, dragging her tongue along the cool mound of sweetness. "Yummy."

"Yummy," Sean repeated.

Patrick grinned at them both, his eyes searching hers until she became addled.

"I'm glad you happened by," he said. "I've been thinking about you."

"Me?"

"You."

"What about?" she asked, puzzled, though she

didn't know why. She thought of him all the time, too.

"About lots of things, but my dad mentioned you the other day."

"Your father?"

"Yes. He said he'd like to see you."

"See me? For what?"

Patrick tilted his head as if he wasn't sure. "I suppose to make amends. Smooth things over."

"There's no amends needed. The situation has been uncomfortable for both of us and I guess I've just—"

"He understands and so do I, but he'd just like to clear the air."

Christie studied his face, wishing she could leap up and say she agreed, but she found it difficult and still had no idea what she was harboring. "We'll see" was all she could come up with.

Patrick shrugged. "That would be nice if you could. It's not just my father that makes me think of you."

That statement sent a jolt through her chest.

He held the cone, looking uninterested in the melting ice cream. "Coming home to Loving has brought back lots of memories."

Christie had her own remembrances—times so difficult and confusing.

"Not the bad times. The good times," he said. "We had a lot of fun back then."

She couldn't deny that. "We did, I suppose."

"Remember the time we left for that wedding, and I guaranteed you I knew where it was."

"How could I forget? By the time we got there, we were the last ones in the receiving line."

Patrick grinned. "I never would stop for directions."

"You didn't like to ask for help back then."

His look bewildered her. Patrick leaned closer and slid his hand across the table near hers. "I still don't, Christie. I've never learned to ask. I even struggle to ask the Lord for help, and I'm not much better at saying things I should."

She wondered if his words held a cryptic message. If so, she missed it.

"I've spent so many years trying to forget my childhood. I'd been hurt so many times. Felt abandoned so many times." He caught a drip on his cone with his tongue, then faced her again, his eyes searching hers. "You know what?"

"What?" she asked, her voice knotting in her throat at the emotion she saw in his eyes.

"You were one of the only people I talked to who seemed to listen and understand." He slid his hand closer and brushed her fingers. "That meant more to me than anything."

The touch sparked up her arm, taking her breath away. "I—I'm sorry I couldn't help you more, Patrick. I'm not sure I understood well enough."

"Not totally, because you had such a stable family. But you tried, and that meant everything." He drew in a lengthy breath and leaned against the chair back.

The absence of his fingers against hers left her wanting more.

"I never told you this," he said. "I was envious of you."

"Envious?"

"Of your family. A mother and father. Something I never had. Every time kids came to school with home-baked cookies for the class, I felt different. I hated the feeling. When I brought treats to school, they were store-bought. Even when kids came from single-parent families, they had a mother. Their dad was the missing parent."

Her heart ached and she could do nothing. She had no idea he'd hurt so badly, and she hadn't known.

"My dad tried," Patrick continued. "He really tried, but it wasn't the same. Mothers do so many little things that fathers don't think to do." He looked at Sean and pulled a napkin from his shirt to blot the ice cream rolling down his arm. "See?"

Christie smiled. "You did good there." But her thoughts drifted back to her own mom and dad. Patrick was right. Her father had slipped her an extra few dollars for her allowance and showed how proud he was with her accomplishments, but her mother had helped her become a woman. They'd baked cookies and talked about girl things. Each parent gave something different to her.

"That's true," she said finally.

"I worry about that for Sean. He needs a mom, but I'm not ready to think along that line yet. I don't know if I ever will be. I've already botched up two marriages."

Concern rose in Christie's mind. How had he botched two relationships? "I realize we both have responsibility for our divorce, but what about your second wife?"

"She had some health problems. Diabetes. She'd had it from childhood. Things got out of control, and—"

"But you can't be blamed for her diabetes and—"

"I can't help but think Sherry's death was God's way of punishing me for messing up our marriage."

"Patrick," Christie said, leaning over to catch his hand. She held it tightly, squeezing his fingers to emphasize sincerity. "Please don't say that. My faith has been pretty feeble lately, but I know God. So do you. The Lord is compassionate and merciful. He doesn't hurt His children any more than you would hurt Sean."

His attention seemed riveted to her hand on his, and Christie longed to pull it away, but she couldn't. She wanted him to know she meant every word, and she loved the feeling of touching him. It had been so long.

After a moment, he shook his head and lifted his

eyes to hers. "I don't know. I've convinced myself of that. It's hard to think differently."

"Maybe you should talk with Pastor Myers."

"Maybe." He wove his fingers through hers and squeezed. "It's good talking to you. I've missed that."

Her pulse tripped along her arm and thudded in her temple. "Please, don't—"

"I'm not asking for anything, Christie. I'd like us to be friends if we could. I'd like that a lot."

She held her breath and closed her eyes a moment. When she opened them, Sean's smiling face covered with chocolate ice cream filled her vision. He seemed the happiest child she'd ever known. Pulling her focus from the boy, she looked at Patrick. "I'd like that, but be patient. It may take time."

"I have all the time in the world," he said.

The heat from their woven fingers rippled up her arm and into her heart.

Chapter Eight

Patrick looked at the calendar. August had arrived too quickly. He'd thought he had plenty of time. He lowered his face in his hands and rubbed his eyes. Yesterday he'd learned that Tammy had cheerleading camp so she'd be busy with school earlier than the rest of the students. Now making plans for Sean's care seemed urgent.

He'd thought about Christie's child care. After they'd talked yesterday, he felt better about their relationship. At least they might be friends. He could ask her about enrolling Sean at Loving Care, but Patrick wanted to wait and see if their reconciliation held up. He didn't want Christie to think he'd mended their relationship for a favor.

Christie was great with Sean. She appeared to like him, but Patrick also knew Christie had wanted a baby and he'd thwarted her plan. Now he felt as if asking her to care for Sean at the center was taking advantage. Maybe he was being foolish for feeling that way, but he did.

He checked the time clock in the storage room. His Friday evening help had arrived, and if he hurried, he might make it to Christie's before she closed the facility. Patrick had wanted to see the place anyway. She seemed so proud of her success. He didn't blame her. Out of curiosity, he'd passed the building a couple of times before he and Christie had smoothed over their differences. The center looked as if it had been a ranch house someone had lived in once, but the location made it perfect for a business. Right on a main road.

Patrick logged off the computer. The rest of the orders could wait until tomorrow, or Monday even. He walked into the restroom, rinsed his face and washed his hands, then ripped off a hunk of paper towel, blotted the water, and threw the toweling into the wastebasket. He checked his hair, ran a comb through it, and was ready.

After a quick word to the evening manager, Patrick slid into his car and headed toward the child-care center. He hoped Christie was still there and as amiable as she had been at the Dairy Dip.

Within minutes, he had parked and stood at the door. He pushed the doorbell.

When the door opened, a young woman scrutinized him a moment. "May I help you?"

"I'm a friend of Christie Hanuman. She told me I could stop by."

The woman glanced over her shoulder. "May I tell her who's here?"

"Patrick Hanuman." He watched her face shift with interest.

"Hanuman? You must be a relative." She gave him a bright smile.

"I'm—I—sort of. Yes."

"I'll see if she's busy."

She closed the door, and he knew it was her way of making sure he was really a friend of Christie's.

A moment later, the door swung open and the girl flagged him inside. "She's in her office." She swung her arm behind her and stepped out of his way.

He headed through the doorway, guessing the room had once been a dining room. Christie sat at her desk and when he entered, she looked up from her work and rose to meet him.

"You finally made it," she said.

Beneath her friendly grin, he recognized tension in her voice. "I hope this isn't a bad time." He glanced toward her desk, wondering if she'd been involved in dealing with a problem.

She hesitated. "Not really." She rubbed the back of her neck, then brightened. "It's a good time. Most of the kids are gone already."

Patrick glanced at his watch. Five-forty-five. As he lifted his head, the doorbell jangled again, and he heard voices behind him. Another parent coming for a child. "Nice place, Christie. I'm impressed."

"Thanks. Would you like to look around?" she asked.

"Sure. Whenever you're ready."

She returned to her desk for a moment, slid some papers into a file, then beckoned him to follow. Stepping through the doorway, he noted a bright cheery kitchen. Small tables and a few high chairs lined the walls opposite the cabinets.

Christie took another door to the hallway, and one by one he viewed the playrooms where two children were still occupied with toys, and an area for naps, he guessed, from the multiple cribs and mats. The rooms were sunny and decorated to appeal to children. He grinned, noticing the staff members followed him with their eyes, subtle, yet curious.

"Really nice," he said. "I'm proud of you."

"Thanks, Patrick." She looked pleased at his comment.

She led the way, and he found himself back in her office again, wondering what to say next. Many things filtered through his mind—how often he had discouraged her from opening a child-care center, how often he had asked her to wait for so many things, how authoritative he must have been. "Looking at all this, I couldn't help but think about how much I discouraged you from doing this."

"I remember."

"I'm sorry, Christie. You were right. A place like

this can be successful.'' Without thinking, he slid his arm around her shoulders and gave her a squeeze.

She didn't pull away, and her response gave him encouragement.

''Can you forgive me?'' he asked, loving the feeling of having her close.

''I'm working on it.'' She tilted her chin upward and sent him a smile.

The familiar scent of her perfume wrapped around him, and Patrick drew a deep breath, inhaling the aroma as if the fragrance would give him the power to keep going.

Realizing he'd held her too long, he slid his arms away from her, avoiding her eyes. He feared she might see the feelings surging through him. Patrick took another look at the room, then faced her. ''How many kids do you have here?''

''Twenty-eight right now. I'm approved for thirty.''

''Then you still have room to expand.''

She shrugged. ''Did you notice the new subdivision being built south of here on Hwy 31? I'm thinking I'll need more space soon.''

''More space? You want to enroll more children? What if someone—''

Her face grew serious as she stepped past him. ''I'm planning an expansion.''

He turned and followed her to a worktable. He

hadn't noticed earlier, but a couple of blueprints lay open on the table.

Christie shifted them toward him and pointed out the features in a businesslike tone he didn't recognize. Her voice rang with surety and reasoned thought. But Patrick hesitated. Why spend money now on a guess? Why not wait until she had to turn people away?

"How long will it take to complete the addition?"

"They said two to three months. I'm guessing longer."

"I would wait on this if I were you. Fill your two slots, and then if you see the demand growing, go for it. I'd hate to see you lose…"

His voice faded as he watched Christie's stance. She'd folded her arms across her chest and stepped back, peering at him with narrowed eyes.

"Why must you always do that, Patrick?" Her words crackled with emotion.

"Do what? I'm just suggesting—"

"Suggesting that you know my business better than I do. I lived with that for seven years. I don't have to anymore."

"I'm sorry. I just thought…" He moved closer, and she moved back. He'd blown it. Messed up their relationship again. His comment had seemed so innocent. He only wanted the best for her.

"If you want a friendship, Patrick, you'll have to learn that this is my business. I've run it for the past five years. It's successful and respected. I don't need anyone to tell me how to do what I already know.''

"I'm sorry. Really sorry." He placed his hand on her arm, but she pulled away. "I'll butt out, Christie. You're right. You've done a great job here. What do I know?''

When she looked at him, her anger had faded, but he saw disappointment in her eyes. Patrick had allowed himself to slip back into his old ways. He'd never been like that with Sherry, but Sherry was different. She liked being the homebody, the passive wife, and he'd loved her, but he hadn't felt the spark that he had with Christie. They'd fought and loved with a passion he'd never experienced with Sherry.

Ashamed at his comparison, he pulled his thoughts to the present. No matter how he'd acted, he did admire Christie's business sense and her accomplishment.

"Thanks for letting me look around. Like I said, you've done a great job. I'm pleased for you.''

"That means a lot to me," she said as her shoulders relaxed. "How are things with you? Your dad?''

"Difficult. He's not well. I see the decline since I've been here this past couple of months, and I can't do a thing about it.''

"I'm sure it's awful. I can't face the day when my folks begin to fail.''

"And there's Sean. I'm worried about him. I have a sitter now, but she's getting ready for cheerleading camp so I'm looking for an alternative." He'd opened his mouth. He might as well barrel along. "How would you like to up your enrollment to twenty-nine?"

Her eyes darkened, and he saw her internal struggle. She released a pent-up breath. "I thought you came to look around as a friend. You should have told me you were a potential customer. I would have given you the full treatment."

"I came as a friend."

"I don't know, Patrick. Under the circumstances, I'm not sure I feel right about Sean being here. It's sort of a slap in my face, isn't it?"

A slap in her face? He'd never meant it to be that.

Christie felt her back tense when Milton slid his arm across her shoulders. She'd wanted to talk with him sooner, but he'd insisted they attend an outdoor concert. He'd been particularly sweet since he'd arrived at her house, but she hadn't found the right time to talk about the topic that burned within her.

"Are you chilled?" Milton asked.

"No. Not at all."

"I thought I felt you shiver," he said, nestling her closer.

She struggled with the desire to pull away. "Would you mind if we leave?" The spoken words startled her.

"Leave?" His concern deepened to a frown. "No, if you're not feeling well."

He stood, and she followed, not wanting to explain her reasons. They hurried down the dark aisle between the benches. The stage lights faded, and the moon spread onto the shadowy path to the car.

Milton unlocked the door, holding it open for Christie to slide in, then he rounded to the driver's side. When he closed the door, he sat a moment before speaking.

"Something's wrong." He shifted to see her, his face furrowing with concern.

Wrong wasn't the word. Something was finally right as far as Christie was concerned. In truth, the answer had come to her over a month ago. How could she commit to one man when another's image brightened her dreams each night and tugged at her heart all day? She could no longer avoid the obvious. Patrick's return had toppled her world upside down.

A yes to Milton would be Christie's spiteful attempt to punish Patrick for remarrying and having the child she'd never had. But she'd stayed close enough to the Lord to know that vindictiveness was not motivation for a marriage. Hurting a kind, caring man like Milton was not her intent and was not what the Lord would have her do. She'd dragged out their relationship far too long.

"Christie, what is it?" He lifted his palm to her cheek and turned her face toward him.

"I'm sorry, Milton. I've made a decision. A decision about us."

He let his hand drop to his lap as if he knew the answer. "I'm willing to wait if that's what you need. I haven't rushed you."

"Time won't change anything, Milton. You're a wonderful man. A catch for the right woman. I'm just not her."

"It's Patrick, isn't it?"

His question startled her, and a rush of heat rose from deep within her stomach and rolled down her limbs. "No. No, it's…" She couldn't help but tell the truth. "It's not Patrick in the way you're suggesting, Milton, but yes, he motivated my thinking."

"What kind of rubbish is that?"

"It's not rubbish. I don't love you, Milton. Not the kind of love that makes a marriage. I admire you. I enjoy your company, and I'm grateful for your friendship. But I fell in love once. Yes, with Patrick. I realize that's over, but the memory of that kind of love tells me that I can never marry you if I'm honest with myself."

He fell against the seat back. "Then, I don't suppose you want this?" He dug into his pocket and withdrew a dark velvet box.

In the dusky light, Christie couldn't see the color—deep blue or red. Maybe black, but she didn't have to open it. She didn't want to open it. Her heart ached at the sadness she'd caused Milton. *Lord, why was I not honest sooner? With him and myself?* She felt hot tears roll down her cheeks and drip onto Milton's hands as he held the box in front of her. "Please forgive me."

He felt the wetness because he withdrew the ring box and wiped his hand against his sleeve. "I had hoped…in time." He clutched the box as if waiting for her to change her mind.

"You deserve someone who can love you fully. I'd be cheating you and myself if I said yes."

"I know you can't have children. I can accept that, Christie. And who knows? Maybe—"

"That's not the problem. It's me. It's how I feel inside." She pressed her palm against her chest. "I have to listen to my heart, Milton."

He lowered his head and slid the box back into his pocket. He adjusted the pocket flap as if in slow motion.

"Can I see you?"

She shook her head, startled that he'd even want to spend time with her. "No. It's best we just end it here."

He sat in silence, staring out the front window while Christie ached for him and for her. Yet, she'd faced the truth. Even if she spent the rest of her life alone, she could never marry Milton. Seeing Patrick with June had left Christie feeling empty until she learned the woman was his cousin. Empty and aware. The incident had forced her to see the truth. She'd finally discerned that marriage without a deep loving commitment was even more lonely and hopeless than being alone. Every day made that more clear.

Then another idea had come to her. Annie's adopting the baby had given her new hope. Christie had heard of single mothers adopting, and with her business well-established, she'd have time to give that consideration. Who needed a man anyway?

Christie uncrossed her legs, then crossed them in the other direction, waiting for her mother to return with the lemonade. Even with the air conditioner the August heat permeated the room.

Today she'd come to break the news that Milton was out of the picture. She could hear her mother now, prying into the whys and hows of it all—questions she wasn't sure she could answer to anyone's satisfaction. The decision was of the heart, not of reason.

"Let me know if it's too sour," Emma said, setting the glass on the side table. She placed hers on a coaster, found another, and then slid one beneath Christie's drink.

Christie watched Emma propel about the room, wishing she'd find a spot and stop moving. She couldn't talk about something so important while her mother was preoccupied.

Emma settled down, brushed a strand of hair from her dampened forehead and let out a stream of air. "Must be humid."

"It is." Christie sipped the cold drink, feeling condensation already dripping from the glass.

"I love it when you drop by unexpectedly," Emma said.

"I would have called, but—"

"You didn't hear me. I *like* it when you don't call. It's like a special surprise." Her mother's warm smile sailed across the distance.

Christie realized she often didn't listen to her parents. Did she think she was too grown-up to pay heed? Not by a long shot. "I saw Dad in the garage."

"He's tinkering, but when he notices your car, he'll be in. You wait and see."

Christie shifted her legs again, wondering if she should drop the brick before or after her father came in. She made her decision, then took another sip of the lemonade. Here goes.

"What a nice surprise." Her father's voice entered the room before he did.

"Hi, Daddy." She rose and met him halfway, planting a kiss on his cheek.

"Why are we so honored?" he asked, settling beside her on the sofa.

This time, she said it. "Besides loving you both, I wanted you to know I broke up with Milton. I realize you both liked him, and I knew you'd be surprised." She barraged them with words, watching their expressions deflate.

"But why?" Emma asked. "He's such a nice man, and he thinks so much of you."

Her father didn't respond. Instead, he studied her.

"That's why, I suppose. I couldn't drag on a go-nowhere relationship. I told you this before. He was getting too serious, and I have nothing to offer him." She didn't add that he really had nothing to offer her, either. Nothing that counted.

"Well, I'm disappointed," Emma said. "You certainly had fun together even if—"

"It's Christie's decision, Emma." Wes gave his wife a telling look. "No matter who we like, Christie has to be the one to decide. I liked Milton myself."

"I do, too, Dad, but I don't love him." She said the words so easily. Why hadn't she realized this before? "Lately I've given it a lot of thought. I realize that love is something I had once, but not now. It's different."

She watched her mother's hopeful expression fade to dismay. "Please don't tell me you're thinking about Patrick again."

Hearing Patrick's name sent heat rising to Christie's face. "No. It's not that."

Emma gave her husband a frantic look. "Wes, talk with her."

Wes shook his head. "Christie's not a teenager, Emma. She's thirty-four."

"Thirty-five, Daddy." Christie clung to the distraction. "I had a birthday a while ago."

"Okay," he said, then returned his attention to Emma. "No matter what age, Christie's old enough to know what she wants to do with her life."

The looks on her parents' faces showed Christie that she needed to plod forward and address their concern. "Listen. I won't lie and say Patrick hasn't thrown my life in a tizzy. Seeing him again has dragged out all the old hurt and anger—the frustration from the divorce. But at the same time, it's reminded me what love really is. I loved Patrick. He made my heart dance and my life wonderful, until…"

"You don't need to explain," Wes said. "Your mom and I know you'll do what's right."

She opened her mouth to continue, but her father hadn't finished.

"And speaking of him, I saw Patrick at the hardware yesterday. He says Joe's not doing well."

Mentioning Patrick's father reminded Christie of his request. "Patrick said his dad wants to talk with me."

"With you? About what?" Emma asked.

Christie lowered her head and looked at the floor. "I haven't talked with him since the divorce."

"Christine, I can't believe that," her mother said.

"Well, it's true. I'm thinking about it."

Emma crossed her arms across her chest and gazed at her daughter. "I should hope so. 'Forgive as the Lord forgives you.' Remember that. Plus the poor man didn't do a thing. It was Patrick, and you're talking with him.''

"Emma," Wes said. "Don't lecture."

Her mother turned away and held her tongue.

"Anyway getting back to Patrick," Wes said, "it nearly broke my heart. He's trying to run that store with his boy underfoot. He told me the baby-sitter went to cheering camp or some such.''

Guilt scuffled up Christie's back as she pictured Sean wandering round the hardware store while Patrick tried to watch him and do his job. He'd asked her a favor, and she'd been horrible. She'd allowed her envy to overshadow compassion. She sat with her head bowed, asking God for forgiveness. How could she be so uncaring?

"It's not right for a child to be in the store," Emma said. "Think of all the things he could get into. I have a mind to volunteer to baby-sit until he finds someone."

Christie sat amazed, hearing her mother's frustration with Patrick shift, in one breath, to her consideration for his child. Still, her parents' concern caught her short while her guilt shifted to shame. She was being selfish not helping Patrick.

Her father looked at her over his glasses. "From what I heard, he hasn't found anyone yet." Too quickly his gaze shifted to Christie. "What's wrong with Loving Care? You're not filled up, are you?"

Chapter Nine

Christie sat outside the hardware store, ready to broach the subject of Sean's enrollment at Loving Care with Patrick. While her pride had nudged her one way for so long, her compassion drove her another. She knew now she needed to apologize to Patrick. After talking with her parents she realized she'd been taking out her frustration with Patrick on Sean. She'd been punishing her ex-husband.

When she'd returned home from her folks' home, Christie had a long talk with herself and with the Lord. She'd taken the Bible from her night stand and opened it at random. She looked at the page and eyed Colossians 3, amazed at the message that almost jumped from the page. *Bear with each other and forgive whatever grievances you may have against one another. Forgive as the Lord forgave you. And over all these virtues put on love, which binds them all together in perfect unity.*

Over all these virtues put on love. Christie remembered her favorite childhood picture of Jesus opening his arms to the children. She certainly couldn't emulate Jesus, but she could do what the Bible asked. Somewhere in her, she had the virtue of love for the innocent child.

The August sun beat through her windshield, and she faced the inevitable. She either had to drive away or go inside the hardware store as she'd planned. She turned off the ignition, feeling the cooler air fade in a breath. Outside, she hit the Remote Lock and headed indoors, reviewing her opening line for when she saw Patrick.

Without asking a clerk, she trudged toward the back of the store, figuring he was doing inventory or setting up stock. Not seeing him there, she reversed her steps until she found a clerk. "I'm looking for Patrick."

"He's not here. Can I help you?"

"I—I'm a friend." She glanced at her watch. "Is he on break?" She pictured him getting a needed moment of peace at the restaurant down the street where he'd taken her.

"No. He was called home by a neighbor. I guess his father is ill."

"His father? Is it serious?"

The man shook his head and shrugged. "I don't

know really. He just scooted out of here like a man on a mission.''

Christie's chest tightened. Patrick needed a friend. She thanked the clerk and hurried from the store on a mission of her own. Although Patrick had requested she talk with his father, she'd not done so. She'd put it off for no other reason than lack of courage. What if something happened today? She would never forgive herself.

She pulled away, her tires squealing in the heavy heat, and headed for Patrick's. In minutes, she turned onto his street and her heart sank. An ambulance sat in front of the house, its lights flashing while neighbors gathered to stare.

Patrick stood beside the stretcher as they settled his father into the vehicle while Sean clung to Patrick's neck, his young face pale with confusion.

Christie parked at the shoulder and hurried toward him. "I just heard," she said. "Is he—"

His surprised expression morphed to one of gratitude. "He looks terrible—gray as ash—but he has help now, and I'm praying he'll be okay."

"I hope so," she said, sending up her prayers for God's mercy. "Can I help? I'll be happy to stay here with Sean."

"You sure?"

"Positive."

"That would be a relief. I hate putting him through all the…"

He let the words slip away and turned to Sean.

"Son, Christie is going to stay with you while I go with Grandpa."

Sean shook his head and buried his face in Patrick's shoulder. Patrick gave Christie a helpless look.

"Let me," she said, stroking Sean's back and whispering assurance to him for a moment before she had Patrick shift him to her arms. The boy wiggled a minute, then rested his head on Christie's shoulder while the ambulance pulled away with Patrick following in his car behind them.

She carried the boy inside the house. Soon they sat on the floor together playing with trucks and educational toys. Christie watched, amazed at the child's coordination and skill. As time passed, the activity shifted to picture books. Sean sat beside her while she turned the pages, telling him the story. When her stomach rumbled, she knew Sean had to be hungry, too, and she made her way to the kitchen to see what she could find to eat.

After spotting a package of ground beef in the fridge, she searched through the cabinets and came up with the ingredients for a meat loaf and baked potatoes, and soon the aroma of dinner drifted into the living room.

She fed Sean and ate a little herself, worrying about Patrick and what had happened. She'd expected him back by now unless... She let her fears ebb away. Instead, she closed her eyes and sent a prayer heavenward. Giving the burden to the Lord eased her.

At eight o'clock, the telephone rang. Christie stared at it, wondering if she should answer or let the machine pick up. Concern gave way, and she lifted the receiver.

"I'm glad you answered," Patrick said. "I'm sorry to keep you waiting so long."

"Don't worry about it, Patrick. How's your dad?"

"They did a catheterization. He has some blockage."

"What will they do now?"

"I don't know for sure. I'd hope to hear something before I come home."

"Is he—"

"Guarded. That's what they call it."

"I'll say another prayer for him."

"I've been praying all evening," he said. "Thanks."

Silence hung on the line for a moment.

"If you need to go home, I can call a neigh—"

"I'm fine." Christie said. "Don't worry about me. Scan's fine. We've had fun playing all kinds of things."

"You'll spoil him," Patrick said.

"No way." She grinned, realizing she'd given the child her undivided attention all evening. "I'll get him ready for bed."

"I shouldn't be much longer."

When she hung up, the day fluttered through her mind like a dream. She had spent the evening playing with Sean, making dinner, and worrying about Patrick's father. She'd never once remembered the circumstances—that Sean was another woman's child, that she hadn't spoken to Joe Hanuman in eight years, that Patrick had stepped out of her life without looking back. It didn't matter.

She moved away from the telephone back to Sean, and finally, she led him up the stairs. After a bath and another story, she put him to bed, sitting beside him a while. A lullaby her mother had sung to her wove through her thoughts and soon the words and tune found their way to her lips. She wouldn't have ever believed she'd be singing to Patrick's son.

Sensing she wasn't alone, Christie glanced toward the doorway and saw Patrick leaning against the doorjamb watching her. Heavy sadness burdened his face, and her fear returned.

She rose and tiptoed to the doorway. She touched his arm. "He's not—"

"No. He's okay. They'll do a bypass tomorrow if Dad's up to it."

"I'm relieved," she said. "You looked so sad when I saw you in the doorway."

Patrick gazed down at her, wishing he could tell her the sadness came from what he'd just seen—his ex-wife singing a lullaby to his son. The image touched his heart with the deepest regret.

He slid his arm around her shoulder. "I can't thank you enough."

She shook her head. "We already said all of that. Are you hungry?"

While she enjoyed the closeness of his embrace, he guided her toward the staircase. "Me? I bet you're starving."

"No. I'm fine. I made dinner for Sean and me. There's plenty there for you."

"You made dinner?" He paused at the steps.

She shook her head. "I know how to cook. Remember?"

He nodded, recalling that she was a good cook. He sniffed the air. "Now that you mention it, do I smell meat loaf?"

"And baked potatoes. I made a salad too." She hurried ahead of him to the first floor.

He watched her bounce with each step, so trim and lovely. She'd always been beautiful. He couldn't imagine how he'd had the courage to leave her.

Then the memories flooded back. He remembered well. His own ugly fears about being a good husband and parent. No one to turn to. Not even God. He didn't know the Lord at all then, but today he did, and he'd bombarded the heavenly Father with continual prayers.

When he reached the kitchen behind Christie, she already had a place set for him at the table and was closing the refrigerator door. Without a pause, she popped a dish into the microwave and motioned for him to sit.

"Want some coffee or tea?" she asked.

"Tea sounds good. I'm saturated with that awful thick stuff from the hospital."

She smiled and set the teakettle on the burner. The microwave buzzer sounded, and before he could say thanks, Christie had set a plate in front of him. The scent of food whetted his appetite, and he forked into the best home-cooked meal he'd had in years, but after downing a few mouthfuls, his curiosity roused him. "I've been wondering how you happened to come here today."

She stood at the cabinet, dropping tea bags into a pot. "I'd stopped by the store."

"You did? Why?"

"Looking for you."

"For me?"

"I had something to tell you, something to talk over."

He spotted a slight flush with her statement. "Okay. I'm all ears."

Christie returned to the table with a mug in each hand. The steam sent a spicy orange aroma into the air as she set the cup in front of him.

She settled into the chair beside him. "I...I wanted to let you know that Sean is welcome at Loving Care. My dad said you've been trying to watch him at the store and that's not safe for him, or easy for you."

"It's been awful." He wiped his mouth with the napkin she'd folded beneath his fork. "Dad mentioned to a neighbor that I was having a bad time so she agreed to help me out today. That's why she was here and gave me a call."

"Talk about little miracles," Christie said.

"If she hadn't been here, Dad would have been dead. I…" Patrick felt tears push against his eyes and struggled to contain them. He hadn't cried in front of anyone in years. Forever maybe, and he didn't plan to start now.

Christie leaned closer and touched his hand. "It's been an awful day, Patrick. Be happy that your dad's in good hands now."

Patrick recaptured his control and nodded. "So was Sean. You've been an angel."

The conversation settled into simple things, and when he finished eating, Christie grabbed up the plates before he could stop her. When he tried to help, she shooed him away. "Go rest. I'll be there in a minute."

He didn't argue. Exhaustion had made itself known long before he'd driven home. Patrick settled on the living-room sofa, enjoying Christie's clanking and scraping in the kitchen. The sound took him back so many years earlier to their home together.

Within minutes, she returned, carrying refreshed tea mugs, but before she sat in a chair, he patted the cushion beside him.

She followed his suggestion without comment,

setting their cups on the coffee table, then leaning back to curl her feet beneath her. She released a sigh and tilted her head against the sofa.

Patrick had all he could do to stop himself from kissing her. He'd always loved her high cheekbones and the generous smile that made her eyes sparkle. Eyes the color of autumn leaves—soft brown with flecks of yellow. Hazel eyes.

He followed her action, stretching his legs out in front of him and leaning his head back as she had done. He let his hand slip from his lap and find hers. She didn't pull away, but curled up more deeply into the sofa.

"This is nice," he said. "I haven't been this comfortable in a long time with anyone. It's so important to have a real friend."

"I know," she said.

Her voice rang with greater meaning than her words said, but Patrick couldn't decipher it.

"Since I've been alone," he said, "I've realized how important life is. Sherry's was cut so short, and I'd like to think God had a reason. It's hope that's kept me from being angry at the Lord."

"I'm just learning that, I'm afraid. After you left, I lashed out at everyone. Everyone but me. I thought I'd been perfect. I know that's not true. It takes two to end a relationship, most of the time."

"Probably not that time, Christie. I know where I went wrong now...now that it's too late."

She seemed to ignore his confession and continued as if he'd said nothing.

"That's why I made a decision recently," she said. "I didn't want to find out I'd made another mistake after it was too late."

He felt her tense, and she turned to him, her face telling him she hadn't meant to utter the words she'd spoken.

"I'm sorry, Patrick. I didn't mean to dump my problems on you. You have enough going on."

He squeezed her hand. "You didn't dump on me. We're talking. That's what friends do." He considered the consequence of asking the question that dangled in his mind, but decided it was worth it. "What decision?"

She sat in silence for a minute, and Patrick feared he'd upset her again, but her answer told him he'd been wrong.

"Milton," she said. "I told him I wanted to stop seeing him."

Patrick shifted on his hip to face her. "You did? How long have you been dating?"

"A year. Maybe longer."

He studied her, wondering what to say. Finally, he took a dangerous step. "Why did you end it, Christie?"

She pressed her lips together a moment before she spoke. "I didn't love him. I liked him. Respected him. But it wasn't love. Love's different. It's deeper and, I don't know, stronger. Love comes from inside your heart and soul. That's how I remember it.''

Her words spiraled through him. That's how she remembered it? Need he ask? ''It's a promise of forever. Except I failed you, Christie.'' He clasped her face in his hands and was lost in her eyes.

She gazed back at him, her eyes searching, a perplexed look on her mouth. A mouth so eager and soft, he remembered. Feeling so right, he followed his heart and kissed her, his memory validated by her pliable, sweet lips, and for a moment, she leaned into the kiss before her hands grasped his arms, and she jerked away.

''No. Stop. We can't do this.'' Her face had filled with panic.

He wanted to ask why, but the answer came loud and clear. Because he'd deceived her once before.

In a heartbeat, Christie rose and grabbed her bag. ''Bring Sean to Loving Care in the morning,'' she said, and vanished through the doorway.

Helpless, he watched her go.

She didn't trust him, and he feared she never would.

Chapter Ten

"Christie."

Christie looked up to see Bev Miller standing inside the doorway.

"Could I talk with you a minute before I leave?"

"Sure." She studied the woman's troubled face, wondering if she were planning to ask for time off. Christie's day had already been stressful. Patrick had dropped off Sean without completing the paperwork for his enrollment and said he'd come by after his hospital visit. Since they would be closing soon, he'd be showing up any minute to pick up Sean.

"This is just a question," Bev said stepping toward Christie's desk. "My mom is moving back to Loving to be closer to us. She misses the grandchildren. Anyway, she's just retired from nursing, and I wondered if you might be able to add someone here, part-time maybe, with those qualifications.''

Christie's mind filled with questions. If Bev's mother needed income, why had she retired? ''She needs to work?'' Christie asked, forming the question so it sounded tactful.

''No. She has a good pension, and she's only a few years from social security. I'm just worried she'll have too much time on her hands. She'll need something to do with herself, and I'm thinking ahead.''

Christie got the silent message. ''She'll be living with you?''

''For a while until she gets settled. I just hate to see her moping around, bored out of her mind. Not to say she won't be a help with the kids. Since I've been alone, it's—''

''You don't have to explain. I understand.'' The vision rose in Christie's mind. If she and her mother lived together, it would be a disaster. Not that she didn't love her mother with all her heart, but Emma's directive nature and Christie's stubborn one would be at blows in a heartbeat.

''So, you're thinking ahead. When is your mother coming to Loving?''

''In a few months. I know the question is premature, but I've been wondering.''

Christie smiled as the expanded facility came to mind. ''We're growing, Bev. Your mother could be a nice addition to the staff. I'd love having a nurse around. Why not talk with me after she gets here?"

Bev backed toward the exit, her face less stressed. "Thanks. I really appreciate it." She gave a wave and hurried through the doorway, her shoulder bumping Patrick as he stepped across the threshold into her office.

"I'm late," he said. "I hope I didn't keep you."

Her chest tightened as he strode into the room, his broad shoulders emphasized by the horizontal stripes of his knit shirt.

"You didn't keep me," she said, avoiding his eyes. "How's your father?"

"So far, so good. They did a triple bypass today, and he's doing okay. It saved his life. The surgeon said the stress on his heart would have been too much for him."

"Then everything happened for the best, even with the scare."

"God works wonders," Patrick said.

She tried to look the other way, fearing he'd sense her riled emotions. Her pulse surged at the memory of his gentle kiss—his mouth against hers, so wonderfully familiar.

Averting her gaze, she rose and pulled out the enrollment forms. "You can sit at the worktable there if you like and complete these." She extended the forms, her free hand gesturing toward the table. "Or just bring them back in the morning."

"Thanks. I might as well do them here."

She felt the papers leave her hand, and she moved across the room to the worktable and rolled the blueprints into a cylinder, clearing a space for him. Seeing the blueprints was a constant irritation. She had finally called the bank and set up the appointment, but she'd lost her spirit for the addition. Was it Patrick's caution that had dampened her enthusiasm? Why should she listen to him? Even the possibility irked her. Christie stiffened her back, determined to call Jeffers tomorrow and get things rolling.

Patrick adjusted a wooden chair in front of the cleared spot at the table. He pulled a pen from his shirt pocket and leaned over the forms. As he worked, Christie watched from behind, enjoying the sight of his back straight and tall. He shifted his weight to pull his wallet from his pocket—his insurance information, she guessed—and she admired his strong hands fumbling with the leather, the familiar movements of his lean body.

Refocusing and bending over her own paperwork, Christie struggled to concentrate. Without permission, her eyes shifted toward Patrick, her thoughts drifting to years earlier before settling on yesterday, then today. The future—she couldn't face it. Not yet.

The chair legs scraped against the flooring, and Patrick's shadow fell across her desk. For the first time, she directed her gaze to his. Her hand trembled as she reached for the documents, then she pulled her attention downward and scanned the forms.

"They look fine, Patrick." She wanted to press her hand against her chest to hold her heart in place. The beating rang in her ears.

Patrick reached behind him and pulled out his wallet again. "I'll pay you now for the first month. Is that right?"

"That's fine," she said. "You can read your options in the information sheet I gave you. Credit cards are welcome, too."

"I have cash," he said, handing her the bills.

Their voices sounded so businesslike—such a paradox from the day before when she had curled up beside him on the sofa, his hand on hers, his lips plying against her mouth. She couldn't bear the loneliness that raced through her limbs and settled in her chest.

"I'm sorry for running off yesterday." The sentence shot from her mouth, surprising her, but she'd said it and felt relieved.

Patrick's face reflected his surprise at her apology. "I shouldn't have done what I did without asking, Christie. It seemed so natural. So right."

"Let's not blame ourselves or each other. It happened. That's the problem of getting too close. Since we have to see each other with Sean here, let's make the best of it."

He nodded. "That's fair. I won't let it happen again."

"Good." She said the word, but while her head agreed, her heart cried no. Fear pitted in her stomach. She was doing something she'd never thought possible. She was falling in love with Patrick all over again.

Patrick leaned back against the uncomfortable hospital chair, watching his father sleep. His color looked bad, and he'd seen the nurses check his vital signs too often for his comfort. But when he asked, they waved it off as normal.

The past week had dragged by. The hospital, the hardware store, the tension with Christie, it all seemed too much. He hated the way things had gone. Why had he kissed her? They'd just made strides toward friendship, and he'd botched it with his unharnessed affection.

He'd acted out of nostalgia. Familiar longings had risen from his bound desire. He hadn't cared about a woman since Sherry died. But now, with Christie around again, everything seemed so good. So directed. So predestined.

He wondered if God were working in his life to bring him full circle. To turn him around and head him back in the right direction. Back home. Not Loving, Michigan, but to loving again. His first love. The love he had promised to cherish until death.

His heart had hardened over the past two years, but in the past weeks, it had opened like his father's bypass, sending warm blood flowing through his veins again, allowing his heart to beat with hope.

In another half hour, he'd return to pick up Sean,

and he'd see Christie again. Each day he struggled to keep his distance, trying to be friendly rather than fawning. It all seemed so hopeless.

Sean's smiling face jigged into Patrick's thoughts. His son had adjusted well to Loving Care. He gave Christie credit for that. The first day when he stepped toward the door, his son had reached out for him, clung to his pant leg, breaking his heart. But despite Christie's feelings about Sean, she'd opened her arms to his son, and before he'd closed the door the first day, he'd seen him in Christie's arms, almost as if he'd already forgotten about his father.

Father. The word roused him, and he rose, eyeing his dad again. He seemed too still. Fear charged up his spine. He stared at his chest, then the monitors. "Dad." Patrick touched his father's arm with a gentle shake. "Dad." Panic flooded him.

"Dad!"

Please Lord. Not yet. Not now.

Christie checked her watch. Only a few children remained, and concern ruffled through her. Patrick was usually here by now. She eyed Sean playing, unaware that his father should have arrived a half hour ago.

When she heard the door bell, she rose and grasped Sean's hand. Preoccupied with the blocks, he grumbled before following her. But the parent wasn't Patrick. The telephone's ring alerted her, and she swept Sean into her arms to catch the call.

She'd grown attached to the boy. He was no more loveable than the rest of the children, but he seemed special. As much as the "other woman" hurt, Sean was part of Patrick.

She lowered the child to the ground and grabbed the receiver. Patrick's voice rasped with alarm.

"Christie. I've run into problems here, and I don't want to leave."

"What is it?"

"Dad's had a cardiac arrest."

"Oh, no," she said, sorrow striking her. "Is he…?"

"No. They've resuscitated him, but he's slipped back into some abnormal rhythm again. I don't want to leave until I know he's okay."

Christie rubbed the back of her neck, feeling his fear. "I understand, Patrick. You should be there. What can I do?"

"I'll give you my neighbor's telephone number— the one who sits with Sean occasionally. Could you call her and see if she could pick him up. It's late, but—"

"Patrick, stop worrying. I'll take Sean home with me. You can come by whenever you feel comfortable leaving."

"I can't do that to you again, Christie."

"Yes, you can." She looked at the boy gazing at her with curious eyes. "Do you have a minute to talk with him?"

"Sure put him on."

She handed the telephone to Sean. He jabbered about nonsensical things, but Christie knew Patrick would be comforted hearing the child's voice.

After a moment, she took the phone and let Patrick get back to his father.

Christie looked down at the child's curious face. "I guess it's you and me, Sean."

He looked at her. "You and me," he said.

The next hour trudged by. She said good-night to her last parent and staff, locked the doors and headed home with Sean in a car seat she kept in a storage room for emergencies.

At home she occupied the boy with some toys she'd brought along from the center while she prepared dinner. Her gaze drifted to the clock, and when eight-thirty came, then eight-forty-five, she tucked Sean into her bed, read him a book, then sang him the lullaby she'd remembered at Patrick's. Another came to mind, and she sang along, making up words when she couldn't remember them. Soon the boy had drifted to sleep, and she rose, relieved.

She'd never experienced having children in her home. Yes, she cared for many at the center with many helpers and all the right equipment. At home, she faced a different situation. Sean had gotten under the sink and found some cleanser, he'd unloaded her cabinet of pans, and he'd dropped his shoe in the toilet. She made a horrible mother.

But Christie loved children, and she could adore Sean so easily if it weren't for—

The doorbell rang, and she tiptoed from the room. When she swung the door open, Patrick stood there, his shoulders bent, his face strained, his eyes tired.

"How's he doing?" Christie asked.

"Better."

"I'm so glad. You look awful."

"Thanks. It's kind of you to say so." He gave her a feeble smile.

She swung the door open wider.

Patrick came inside and crumpled into a chair. "I can't take this stress much longer. If I had siblings…someone to spend time at the hospital, but I don't, and I don't want to leave Dad there without family."

"I know. It's difficult." She had been family once. She would have been at Patrick's side, or taken turns so they could each rest. Tension showed on his face, and her heart ached. "Is he conscious?"

"On and off. He's sleeping a lot."

"Can I fix you something to eat?"

"No. Thanks. The nurse gave me a sandwich while I waited." His mouth curled faintly at the corners. "And some of that famous hospital coffee."

"Are you sure? I can make you some fresh coffee."

He nodded. "I need sleep, that's all."

"Sean just drifted off a few minutes ago."

Patrick eyed his watch. "I hate to disturb him."

"Once he's sound asleep, he'll probably stay that

way.'' She moved closer. ''Want to rest a while on the sofa? I'll bring you a pillow.''

''You're too good to me, Christie. I'd better stay awake, or you'll never get rid of me.''

Part of her wished that were the case. She'd love to wake up in the morning and see Patrick's face, his whiskers peeking from his chin, his hair tousled and his eyes heavy with sleep. The memories wrapped around her, dragging out a desire she'd kept bound inside her. She missed being a wife. She longed to be a mother. Even her endometriosis couldn't dampen the feeling.

Patrick rose and gestured toward the hallway. ''He's in your room?''

''It's right down the hall.'' She led the way and stood in the doorway while Patrick lifted the boy in his arms and kissed the top of his head. Sean gave a faint moan, but remained asleep.

The scene touched her heart. Father and son. A love so pure and precious. She stepped back as Patrick maneuvered his weighted arms through the doorway.

At the front door, Christie put her hand on the knob and captured Patrick's gaze. ''You can't go on like this. Let me take a turn.''

''You take a turn?'' His eyes narrowed.

''Tomorrow after work, I'll bring Sean to the hospital, and you can take him home while I sit with your dad. You need to spend time with your son, and you need to rest.''

"That's kind to offer, but you haven't talked with my dad in years and—"

"And it's about time I did."

He studied her, tenderness written on his face. "Are you sure?"

"You couldn't stop me."

Before she could think, Patrick leaned over and pressed his lips to hers. She opened her eyes and studied his tired but tender face. Without a moment's hesitation, she lifted her hand to his roughened cheek and felt the growth of whiskers. "I'll see you tomorrow."

He turned his mouth and kissed her hand. "Thank you."

Patrick stepped outside, his son nestled in his arms, and Christie watched them go, her vision blurred by tears of sadness. She loved him. But could she forget the hurt? Could she trust him or her heart?

She didn't think it was possible.

Chapter Eleven

Christie sat with Sean in the hospital waiting room, and in a few minutes, Patrick came through the doorway.

"Hi," he said, the strain still evident on his face. "How's my boy?" He leaned down and brushed Sean's cheek.

"Grandpa's sick," he said, a look of concern marring his childish features.

"He is, but he's getting better, so don't worry." Christie asked the question with her eyes.

"His rhythm is back to normal, and his pulse is strong. That's all we can ask for," Patrick said.

"I'm glad to hear it." She brushed her fingers against Sean's shoulder, knowing she had to go, but wishing she could stay. "Does he know I'm coming?"

Patrick nodded. "He does."

"And?"

"He's pleased. Don't worry."

"Then I suppose I should go in."

"Room fourteen. It's cardiac care so he's alone in the room. He does have a window." He grinned. "Great view of the parking structure."

She stepped toward the door, and he caught her hand. "Thanks."

"Get some rest. I'll stay for a couple of hours." She patted her shoulder bag. "I brought a book to read if he sleeps. If anything goes wrong, I'll call you."

"See you later, Sean," she said, bending down to his level.

The child wrapped his arms around her neck and gave it a squeeze. "See you yater."

She grinned at the lost *L* as she stepped away. Though she wanted to look back, she propelled herself forward. In the hallway, Christie hit the large button on the wall, and the double doors swished open. Moving along the glassed cubicles, she avoided looking inside, not wanting to face the critical patients who lay there uncertain of their fate.

She checked the room numbers. Ten. Eleven. She turned her head to the left. Fourteen. Christie stopped and released a deep sigh before forcing herself through the doorway.

The curtain around the bed was drawn, blocking her view, but she looked through the window and noticed the parking structure. She smiled, thinking of Patrick. She paused at the gap in the privacy curtain and took a another breath for courage before stepping inside.

She was unprepared for the assembly of monitors and tubes and it set her back on her heels. Patrick's father breathed softly, his head turned away from her. Christie stood beside the bed and wondered what to do. Should she wake him or sit and wait? She eyed the lone uncomfortable chair against the wall. Making her decision, she took a step backward.

"Christie?"

Joe's voice startled her.

"Yes," she said, moving closer. "I thought you were sleeping." She rested her hands against the bed railing. "Patrick just took Sean home."

"Good. He's been here too long, hovering over me like an old woman."

The humorous analogy made her smile. "He's been worried."

"I know," he said. "How are you?" He shifted his body to face her more directly.

"I should ask that of you. How are you feeling?"

His mouth lifted at the corner, and she heard a quiet chuckle. "Just glad to be here from what I understand."

"You had a bad time," she said, knowing that she was avoiding the inevitable.

"Looks like I'll live."

"That's the latest I've heard." Words of apology sat on the tip of her tongue, but she hesitated. Dad. She'd always called him Dad. Joe. She struggled with her indecision, then decided to avoid addressing him as anything.

"I'm glad you came," he said.

Patrick's father had opened the door, and she welcomed it. "Me, too. It's been too long. I'm sorry for my neglect. The situation was so hurtful and—"

His gnarled hand reached upward and touched her fingers. "You don't have to explain. I was as much at fault as you. Mine was embarrassment for my son's neglecting you."

He ran out of breath, and Christie slipped her hand over his, assuring him. "Don't talk. You need to rest."

Joe didn't pay heed. "I knew it was Patrick's fault. You'd been a good wife. He had no one to learn from. No mother to teach him what to expect from marriage. I was useless. I didn't know a thing."

"Please, Dad..." The word had slipped out, but it felt good, and she thanked the Lord for giving her the gumption to address him from her heart. "Please don't worry who's to blame. It's not important." She shifted her hand and laid it against his fingers. "I'm going to stay for a while, and I want you to rest."

She slipped his hand back to the blanket and gave

it a pat. "Want some water? I see they have some here with a straw."

He nodded, and she lifted the plastic cup closer and let him draw a few sips. Water dripped from his chin, and she brushed it away with her fingers, feeling the stubble of whiskers just like she'd felt on Patrick the night before.

Christie placed the cup back on the tray and stepped back. "I'll be right here if you need me."

He'd already closed his eyes, and she settled onto the stiff chair before sliding her novel from her bag. She moved around so the light from the window hit the pages, but her mind didn't settle on the story printed on the pages. Instead, the older man's words filled her thoughts. *I knew it was Patrick's fault. You'd been a good wife.* She'd lived that lie too long. One day, she'd need to tell Patrick how she'd contributed to the divorce—how she'd made no effort to save it, but had driven him away. The guilt was hers as much as his, but it would take courage to confess. She felt so ashamed.

She listened to Joe's steady breathing, knowing they had lots to talk about. Complete healing would take time, but she prayed it would happen. She closed her eyes and asked the Lord to show mercy on the man she'd avoided for these past years.

Two men, really. She'd let hate and bitterness swallow her so she couldn't see out of the darkness. Like Jonah and the whale, she thought. But the light had returned. No matter what happened, she would have to tell Patrick the truth one day.

Patrick felt uplifted. His father's recovery, though slow and not yet complete, had been a gift from God. He'd be coming home from the hospital tomorrow if all went well.

He'd been so grateful to Christie. Despite the bad times they'd had, when he needed her, she was there, and on top of it all, she'd been wonderful to Sean. He owed her so much. More than he could ever repay. But tonight, he hoped to show her that he appreciated all she'd done.

Patrick slid from his car and headed up the walk, his feet crunching the autumn leaves that had drifted to the sidewalk. Lately the Loving Care sign gave him a warm feeling. He knew Sean was receiving loving care, and he felt closer to Christie.

He rang the bell, and a woman he'd learned was Bev answered the door. She gave him a friendly smile. "Sean's in the playroom. I'll get him."

"Is Christie busy?" he asked.

She waved him toward her office. Assuming Christie was free, he turned to her office and stood in the doorway. The telephone was pressed against her ear, and he stood back, not wanting to intrude.

"Yes. I've spoken to the bank, but I'm still thinking," she said, a frown furrowing her forehead. She shook her head. "No. I haven't contacted another construction company. I want to make sure this is what I want to do. We're talking about a lot of money here.''

Patrick took a step back from the door. He longed to head into the room and tell Christie to stand her ground and say no. The man was obviously pushing her, and in Patrick's opinion, she shouldn't add on to the building until she had kids spilling out the doors…but he stopped himself. They'd dealt with his meddling before. He had to learn.

When he heard the receiver hit the cradle, he moved forward and gave a rap on the doorjamb.

The strain left her face, and her eyes brightened as she rose. ''How's your dad?''

''Coming home tomorrow, I hope.''

''That's great news.''

She looked so lovely today. Maybe it was the color of her attire, dark green slacks and a knit top with shades of tree leaves touched by autumn—the same colors he'd seen on the way to Loving Care. ''Nice outfit,'' he said, letting his thoughts surface as words.

''Thanks.''

He grasped the moment while he had courage. ''Do you have plans for tonight.''

''Not me. I'm going straight home.''

''Is that a must?''

She frowned, studying his face. ''Are you asking if I have to go home?''

He nodded. ''I thought maybe you'd like to go to dinner and catch a movie.''

She tilted her head. "What about Sean?"

"My neighbor's sitting for me. What do you say? It's been a couple of weeks since I've had a chance to enjoy an evening out and once Dad's home..." He looked at her expression and could almost hear her thoughts. "Dinner. Movie. That's it."

"Sure. That would be nice."

Relief shuffled over him. "Great."

"But on one condition," she added.

His confidence dropped a foot. "What's that?"

"You pick the restaurant. I pick the movie."

His concern vanished. "A chick flick. Right?"

She only grinned.

Christie pushed someone's popcorn box aside and worked her way between the rows of seats to the aisle. She wondered why people didn't carry their trash to the nearby wastebaskets.

"Did you enjoy the picture?" Patrick asked, catching up to her as they moved through the double doors.

"I cried, didn't I?" She loved watching his face light with a smile. For so many days during his father's illness, his smile had taken a vacation—a luxury he needed for himself.

They stepped outside into the autumn evening air. The scent of dried leaves and moist earth replaced the buttery aroma of the theater. Christie's shoulder brushed against Patrick's arm, reminding her how much she had enjoyed the feel of his skin against hers as they shared the same armrest during the movie. The awareness had lured her attention from the screen more than once.

But the emotion frightened her, too. Their friendship had stabilized, even grown during the past weeks of his father's illness. The night breeze whipped around the building, and a chill shivered through her. Or hadn't it been the breeze that caused the sudden shiver?

Patrick moved closer in the dim light and slid his arm around her shoulders. "Cold?" he asked.

"A little," she said, fighting the lingering doubts in her mind. Patrick had stepped back into her life and aroused her longing, just as he had years ago when they were young. She'd walked into their marriage starry-eyed, but she'd soon learned that stars blocked reality. Marriage wasn't a fairy tale. It was real.

"You're quiet," he said as they neared the car.

She shrugged, unwilling to verbalize the muddled feelings that filled her. She felt like a pulley, heading in one direction, then another, never knowing at which end she would stop.

Patrick unlocked the door and held it open while she slid in. In a moment, he'd climbed in the other side and stuck the key in the ignition, but he didn't turn it.

"Something's bothering you," he said.

She sat a moment, trying to decide what it was

that had put her on edge. "I don't know. I'm scared."

"Why?" He leaned closer, resting his arm across the back of the seat. "You're not afraid of me, are you?"

"Not of you, Patrick. Of us." The truth had caught her unaware.

"I don't understand. We're getting along great. It's like old times."

His voice trailed off, and she figured he'd had the same thought she did. "But it's not. Is it?" she said. "It's a new time, and a new situation. We've matured and grown in new directions. The two people who fell in love years ago aren't here anymore."

"That's not true. We're the same. In here." He tapped his chest, his gaze riveted to hers.

She saw desperation in his eyes. "No we're not. I wish we were, because I could so easily fall in love with you again, but I can't and that's what's bothering me."

"Why not? Why not let it happen? I feel the same."

"Because I'm afraid when the stars fade, and the sun rises, we'll be right back in the same boat that we were in. Except now it's more complicated. You have Sean. We—I don't want to hurt him."

"I know you care about him, Christie. I see it in your eyes. I watch how you treat him. Like a mother."

Her heart sank as the truth smacked her between

the eyes. "But there's the problem. I'm not his mother. You walked out the door one day looking for something. I don't know what. You left because you didn't know how to love. But once away from me, you found it. You had the child that I wanted so badly. Can you understand how that hurts?" She pressed her trembling hand against her chest, feeling her heart hammer beneath her palm.

"Christie, please. I know I was wrong. I realize what I did. It was horrible. I had to grow up and find my faith. I did that. I'm ready to be a husband."

"But I don't know that I'm ready to be a wife and mother. I'm afraid that we're slipping back into the old mold. That we're fooling ourselves into thinking that we've patched up the past. But have we really? Can I be confident in you, Patrick? Can I trust you? Right here?" She slammed her hand against her chest, feeling the sting through the cloth. "I wish I could say yes, but..." Tears welled in her eyes and rolled down her cheeks.

Where the discussion had come from she didn't know, but it had lain in her heart for so long. She loved Patrick. She knew it. But she couldn't tell him, because it was a love that couldn't be.

"It's Sean, isn't it?" He shook his head and fell back against the seat. "I can't do a thing about my child, Christie. He's my son and I love him with all my heart. I loved his mother once. Not the same kind of love I had with you. That was different. A first love. That only happens once."

She remembered the early years. They were wonderful, but suddenly the wall came up. ''You're forgetting, Patrick.'' The private world she couldn't penetrate. The look in his eyes as if he were miles away in a place she couldn't even put her little finger.

''I know. We had a love that wavered from passion to pain. Desire to despair. We were kids, and our love was raw. But not anymore, we know what makes a marriage now. I wish you could love my son for who he is, not for who his parents are.''

''Stop. Please.'' Her emotions spiraled. How could she deny her feelings for the boy? She cared for him deeply. She— Reality struck her. He was the child of Patrick's other love. She knew it was selfish and horrible, but the feeling was there.

''You expect me not to have feelings for you?'' he asked. ''I can't.''

''I don't expect anything. I…'' Christie had nothing more to say. She felt empty and wounded. Her heart ached with confusion.

''Time,'' Patrick said, leaning closer, brushing her hand with his fingers. ''Let's take our time. I keep feeling like the Lord brought me back to Loving for more than my dad. I don't know what providence is exactly, but I really believe that we've been brought back together for a reason. Please give us time. Don't push me away.''

His words hung in the air. *Don't push me away.*
He'd pushed her away once. If she took a chance,
would he do it again?

For the next two weeks, Christie struggled with
her dilemma. She blamed Patrick for pushing her
away once, and the truth was she'd done as much
pushing as he had. But hers had been worse. She'd
known what she was doing.

Patrick had asked for friendship now, and it had
grown, but always, beneath their new relationship,
Christie had dealt with guilt, remembering what
she'd done and knowing she had to ask Patrick's
forgiveness.

She eyed the clock. Nine-fifteen. He'd be home
from the hardware store by now, and the babysitter
would be gone. She had to tell him the truth while
she had the courage. It was now or never.

Her hand shook as she zippered her warm jacket
and climbed into the car. She'd thought of calling,
but what would she say? *I want to come over to
make a confession.* By the time she heard Patrick's
voice on the other end of the line, she would have
chickened out. Welched on her own decision. Christie knew herself too well.

Admitting her part in the failed marriage meant
admitting she wasn't perfect. Perfection. She'd lived
with the attribute her whole life. It had dominated
her thinking, twisted her desires, thwarted her creativity.

Outside, the cool wind whipped against her and

sent a shiver down her back. The wind or fear? She climbed into the car, turned on the lights, and backed out of the driveway.

The night was dark, the moon hidden behind a heavy bank of clouds. Too soon for snow, she thought. In northern Michigan snow fell in September, but not in Loving. Still the sky looked dark and dire, matching the feeling inside her.

When she pulled up to Patrick's, she turned off her lights and sat at the curb, grasping courage. She had come to tell the truth, but she realized the truth had become a mountain, a confession so big it shamed her.

She climbed the porch steps and rang the doorbell, wishing she could turn back and give this more thought.

The porch light flashed on, and the door swung open. Patrick's surprised face eased to a welcome. "Christie. Come in."

He pushed the door wider, and she entered the small foyer, feeling the warmth strike her icy flesh.

"Is something wrong?" Patrick asked, holding his hand out for her coat.

She shook her head. For a moment, she wanted to cling to her jacket to make a quick escape, but she relinquished it and was relieved when he hung it on a hook beside the door where she could get it easily.

"I'm having a late dinner. Care to join me?"

"No. I just came by for a minute."

He beckoned her into the kitchen and headed for the counter. She realized he was making her a cup of tea, and she sank into a chair at the table and waited. The scent of orange spice greeted Christie when he set the cup in front of her.

"Thanks," she said, hearing her voice catch in her throat.

He sat, picked up the fork and dug it into a spaghetti mixture. "So why this pleasant surprise?"

His lighthearted tone bounced into her thoughts like a balloon she was about to prick with her pointed confession. "It's not pleasant, Patrick. I want to talk about something that's been bothering me. Something that I should have told you long ago."

His friendly grin sank to a frown as the fork slipped from his fingers. "What is it?"

Christie jumped at the clank of metal against the plate. "You've asked us to be friends and I've struggled with that, though I like the closeness I feel." She swallowed her desire to evade the truth. "Part of my reticence is guilt. I've let you take the blame for our divorce when I was as much a part of it, if I'm honest."

"I don't understand," Patrick said, leaning closer as if his nearness would help his comprehension. "How were you to blame?"

"I didn't help you, Patrick. I didn't have the patience. I didn't take time to listen to what you needed. You were muddying my fairy-tale marriage.

I turned away from you. You know how I withdrew. I was no longer the Christie you married.''

''Yes, but I thought that was my doing. I'd let you down.''

Tears moistened her eyes. ''No. I let you down. I knew you were struggling with issues, but I didn't want your problems to sully our perfect world. I wanted you to get over it without my having to deal with it. I felt sorry for myself. I wanted my own business and a child. You didn't share my dreams, and I pushed you away, physically and emotionally.''

''Months ago I told you why,'' Patrick said. ''I was so afraid I'd fail you and a child as a husband and father. I'd never realized the responsibility of making a marriage work. I'd never seen it in my own home, but that's an excuse. I didn't know the Lord and what the Lord expected. It was the easy way out. The easy way for me. But it wasn't easy, Christie. I grieved as much as if you'd died.''

''I had died before you left. I'd pulled myself away from you. I'd shut the door and withdrawn from you in every way rather than opening my arms and admitting we were both needy. I'm ashamed of myself.''

''I was hurt. I'll admit that. I saw you distancing yourself. I knew you avoided me. I felt your coldness toward me, but I thought it was my fault. I thought—''

"You thought wrong. I didn't give you a chance."

He pushed against the mug handle, turning the cup one way, then the other, his eyes glazed with thought...with her confession.

"When did you realize what you had done?" Patrick asked.

The truth lay like a lump in her throat, choking her. "Always."

"You mean you planned it? You acted that way knowingly?" His jaw sagged with his question.

"I wanted to get even with you for messing up my life. I wanted you to beg me to be my old self. It didn't work."

"Then why didn't you give up when it failed? You could have told me. Instead, you let me think... I thought I'd..." His words faded, and a look of anger sparked in his eyes.

She shuddered at the look in his eyes. Cold and bitter, the way she'd felt once. "When you needed me, I wasn't there."

Christie rose and grasped the chair back to steady herself. "Now it's your turn, Patrick. Can you trust *me* ever again? Can you forgive *me?*"

She didn't wait for an answer. She grabbed her jacket and dashed through the door.

Chapter Twelve

"What can I get you, Dad?" Patrick studied his father resting in the recliner. Though his skin color had returned to normal since he'd come home from the hospital, his father's health had a way to go.

"Some decent food," he said. "I'll never get my strength back if you keep feeding me frozen dinners."

Trying to remain good-natured, Patrick ignored the comment. He'd been on edge since Christie had walked out the door, taking his heart with her. He was doing the best he could. Between running the business, keeping the house together, caring for his dad and Sean, Patrick had little time to prepare home-cooked meals.

"I'll see what I can do," he said, making his way

to the kitchen, more for his own reprieve than for his interest in cooking.

Patrick sank into a chair and thought. Christie had thrown him off course, and he couldn't get her out of his mind. At first he'd been angry. Later, frustration took over. Why hadn't she told him earlier? She'd had a couple of months to clear the air. They could have dealt with the hurt and moved ahead. He'd tried to prove himself, tried to show her the man he was now, and he thought he knew her. But he didn't.

Until a couple of weeks ago, he'd been confident they had made strides toward mending their relationship. He had wanted nothing more, but now she'd hurt him with her confession. It wasn't what she'd told him, but that she'd kept it secret for so long since they'd met again. He'd opened his heart, and she'd kept quiet. Why hadn't she told him the truth? He could have handled the truth before. But now?

In the hallway, Patrick listened up the stairs to make sure Sean was still sleeping. He'd been whiney and listless. Patrick hoped Sean wasn't coming down with something.

Hearing only quiet, Patrick entered the kitchen and moved to the refrigerator. He stared inside. Nothing looked appetizing. He closed the door and opened the freezer. Frozen dinners. That's all he had in the house and all he had energy for making. His father would eat one or starve.

Sighing, he shut the door and rubbed his face. Carry-out. They could have pizza or chicken. Sean would love the pizza. His dad, the chicken. Hating to go out again, he headed for the telephone to call in an order, thinking it was that or—

The doorbell stopped him. He checked his watch. Christie. Could it be? She'd be on her way home about now. His pulse picked up speed. Maybe she'd had second thoughts...or third.

He made his way to the front door. Seeing the visitor through the screen, he faltered. "Mrs. Goodson, what a surprise."

Christie's mother stood on the porch, a container clutched in her hands. "Don't just stand there. Open the door so I can bring in this casserole."

"Food?" He lifted his eyes to heaven, wondering if this was God's answer to his need.

"I figured your father could use a good meal."

Amazed, Patrick pushed open the screen, holding it while Emma came through the doorway. He tilted his head toward the kitchen, and she went ahead.

"You're a godsend," he said, following her, then standing in the doorway watching her put the casserole on the counter.

"I guessed you've been eating TV dinners or carryout so I decided to bring you a home-cooked meal."

Patrick's heart warmed at her kindness, but then he wondered if she knew about his situation with Christie. Emma had always been civil to his father, but Patrick continued to feel the strain between himself and her. Could she ever forgive him? "Dad was just moaning that he wanted something edible for a change. He's in the living room. Go say hello."

"Pop this in the microwave for a few minutes." She turned to gaze at the timing buttons. "Try the Warmup Sensor. Then add another minute." She left the casserole on the counter and disappeared through the doorway.

Patrick stood a moment, studying the button she'd indicated. Confident he knew which one to use, he took a peek at the casserole. Something with noodles and chicken. It was still warm and the scent drifted upward past the lid and whetted his appetite.

Emma's voice drifted in from the living room, punctuated by his father's deeper voice. He let them talk a moment while he found a can of vegetables, then the can opener. Not fresh, but he hoped, tasty.

Figuring he should be hospitable, Patrick put on the teakettle. If his memory served him right, Emma liked tea. By the time, he found the tea bags and pulled out the cup, the whistle had given a trill. He finished the brew and carried it into the living room.

"I made you a cup of tea," Patrick said, setting it on the table nearest Emma.

"Thank you," she said, patting the cushion beside her.

He peered at her invitation to sit, puzzled as to her true motivation for the visit. Was it his father or him she'd really come to see?

Patrick sat beside her, listening to the conversation, but soon his father's words faded, and he realized his dad had drifted off. "Sorry. He still needs his rest."

"It's not your father I wanted to talk with anyway," Emma said. Her look left no doubt she'd come to see him.

Patrick shifted, feeling nervous all of a sudden like a child ready to be punished. "You want to talk with me?"

She nodded.

He waited, wishing he could vanish and sorry he'd come in with the teacup. He'd guessed her visit was twofold. Christie must have told her something.

"I'm worried. I guess that's how to say it," Emma said.

"Worried? About my father?"

Her faint grin softened her serious face. "Well, him, too, I suppose, but about Christie and you."

"What about us?" The words left him, and he realized his avoidance was stupid. "You mean about our talk?"

This time her face became puzzled. "Your talk?"

"You mean Christie didn't tell you?" Obviously she hadn't or Emma would have been honest.

"I'm not sure what you talked about unless it was about mending your relationship." She gave him a wary look.

Finally, he understood. Naturally she worried about her daughter getting tangled up with him again. "You mean you're afraid I'm trying to sweet-talk her back into a relationship."

"Something like that."

She took a sip of the tea, then set the cup down with a ting as it hit the saucer.

Why tell her about their talk? Why go there when Christie hadn't? "You know Christie well enough to know I can't sweet-talk her into anything. She's glued to her convictions. I only asked to be friends." He couldn't tell her the whole truth.

"It's hard to be friends when you've treated the person as an enemy. Why should she trust you, Patrick? What's different?"

A great deal was different now. But Emma had asked about what had changed him, and he wanted to tell her. "Do you want the full story or the short version?"

"Let the casserole get cold," she said. "The full story is more important."

He began slowly, struggling to find the right words to explain his feelings and fears. He talked about finding the Lord, then about finding Sherry, and how his life had changed for the better. Having God in his life had eased his worries, softened the hurt he'd felt from childhood, wondering if he'd caused his mother to leave, wondering why he wasn't loveable and wishing he were like the other kids. Unable to quench the fear he'd had for so many years, he'd walked out on Christie and avoided dealing with his past.

And what was he doing now? He'd turned on Christie as quickly as she'd turned on him—without thought, without hope, and without forgiveness. God's Word filled his thoughts. But hope that is seen is no hope at all. *Who hopes for what he already has? But if we hope for what we do not yet have, we wait for it patiently.*

Patience. Hope and patience. If he could forgive Christie, then she could forgive him.

"Please understand that I had never blamed Christie for our divorce," he said, cloaking what he'd learned from Christie's admission. Why weight Emma with those problems? "I thought it was me. I'd given up. I was the one who'd feared failure as a parent and who lacked confidence to be a good husband." The error of his ways struck him for the first time. "But I never told her."

"Why didn't you talk to her, Patrick?" Emma asked.

Why hadn't he? If he had, Christie might have been honest. Honesty could have saved their marriage. If he'd been open, Christie might have told him then what she was doing to push him away.

He wrestled to find an answer for Emma that made sense. Something reasonable. Back then, he'd not been a man of logic or reason. The truth struck him. "I didn't tell her because it made me look weak. I was the man of the family. I was cocksure of everything—our life, our finances, everything.

But inside, I was so afraid that I'd be like my mother. She ran out on us when I was a kid.''

Emma's expression changed. Her narrowed eyes became tender and moisture misted her gaze. She rested her hand on his arm. ''I know.'' Her voice was as gentle as a feather wafting on a breeze.

''I watched my dad suffer,'' Patrick said. ''Then after all my worry, I did the same. I did run away like my mother had done.'' The words, the awareness flattened him like a steamroller.

''Not exactly,'' Emma said. ''You didn't leave a son behind to be wounded by your actions. Your mother did that.''

That was the only saving grace he could think of. He hadn't left behind a bewildered child wondering what he'd done to make his father run off. ''But I hurt Christie, and I'm so sorry for that.''

''Thank you for your honesty. I feel better having heard your side of the story.'' She gave his arm a squeeze. ''Really.''

Her presence took him back. Until the divorce, Emma had been the mother he didn't have. He missed her, too. ''Thanks. I needed someone to hear me.'' And he needed Christie to hear him, too. Hope. Patience. Forgiveness.

Emma rose, lifting the teacup and saucer from the table. ''It all had a reason, Patrick. I think you know what that was.''

He stood as she had done, wondering what she meant.

Without explaining, she carried the china to the kitchen. He followed her to the doorway. "What could be good about what happened?"

Her loving eyes misted with a mother's tears. "You found the Lord. Sometimes we go through tribulation and sorrow because it leads us home. It leads us to Jesus."

"That was a big price to pay," Patrick said, thinking there might have been an easier way.

"Not as big a price as Jesus paid for you and me." She patted his arm. "Now heat up that casserole."

She whisked past him, and before he could let her out, he heard the screen door slam, and her footsteps fade down the porch steps.

Christie looked at the blueprints she'd pushed to the back of the worktable. She had let the negotiations for an addition drag on for months, and now Jeffers Construction was pressing for her answer.

She could picture the children playing in the sunny new room, the toys and books on shelves lining the walls. The old rooms would give her more space for naps and an extra "quarantine" spot for sick children.

Christie had experienced the problem of ailing kids, and she liked the idea of having a special place for ones who become ill during the day. She'd explained to herself over and over the reason for wanting the addition. If Patrick hadn't come into her life, she would have signed the contract, and the construction might be nearly completed.

Resentment snaked up her spine. Then the truth snapped her back to reality. When had she listened to anyone, especially Patrick? She'd faltered on her own—worrying about the cost and her rationale. Patrick might have been right. She'd accused him of meddling, but he'd given her sound advice. She heard about a new child-care center opening on the opposite side of town. That could cut into her present business. What would she do then?

"Why so serious?"

Christie turned toward Annie. "Thinking," she said.

"Shouldn't do that. It'll get you into trouble." Annie stepped closer, a smile growing on her lips. "Next week, I'll be a mother."

"Annie," Christie said, throwing her arms around her friend. "I'm so excited."

"I want you to be one of my first visitors."

"You name the date, and I'll be there." Joy filled Christie's heart and vibrated through her like a celebration, and for once envy hadn't come to the party. She truly rejoiced for Annie and Ken's blessing.

When the doorbell chimed, Annie gave her a parting hug and hurried from the room to answer the door.

Annie's joy filtered into Christie's thoughts. Annie's life had taken on new meaning, as Christie's had when Patrick had come back into her life.

To her surprise, Christie felt renewed. She needed to ask Patrick's forgiveness. She'd walked out on him, not letting him vent his anger. He deserved that, and she deserved to take it standing up. They'd both made mistakes, but they'd both grown. She'd put so many blocks in their way. Time now things changed.

Christie gave a last look at the blueprints and pivoted as a figure in the doorway caught her attention. She looked up to see Patrick as if her thoughts had brought him here. He stood with one hand behind his back, a boyish look on his face.

"Hello," she said, finding her heart in her throat.

"I have a peace offering."

She didn't respond, realizing she was the one who should have brought a peace offering.

Patrick listened to her silence a moment, then moved closer. "Okay. It's really a friendship offering. I want to step back and start again."

Start again. "Patrick, I want to apologize for—"

He lifted his hand to stop her while his other hand jutted forward holding a shiny gold box wrapped with gauzy green ribbon and topped with an autumn leaf. Christie eyed it.

"It's for you." He moved closer.

She managed to pull her gaze from his and look at the package. He set it in her hands. Candy. She eyed the discreet label on the side. *Jenni's Loving*

Kisses. She wanted to be lighthearted and not let him know the emotion that wrested inside her. "What about my figure?"

"It looks good to me," he said, then shaking his head as if he realized he'd taken one step beyond friendship already. "You can share it with the staff." He tilted his head toward the doorway.

"Thank you," she said, distraught at feeling such pleasure in his gift. After all that had happened between them, he was offering her another chance.

Though she hated to ruin the lovely packaging, Christie pulled off the ribbon and peeked inside. Dark and milk chocolate bonbons sat in the box, each decorated with a different swirl or colored topping.

"My neighbor has her own in-home business making those things. They're good. Try one."

She lifted out a peace offering and let her teeth sink into the creamy chocolate. Her taste buds awakened with an unusual spicy flavor—cinnamon. "Delicious." She extended the box toward Patrick. "Have one."

He shook his head. "Those are for you."

"I won't share them," she said, giving him a forgiving smile. She licked her fingers, savoring the last bit of flavor. She caught his steady gaze. "So. ?"

"I'm here to pick up, Sean…and to—"

"Bring a peace offering."

He shrugged, sending her another boyish smile. The cleft in his chin deepened, and an unexpected sensation rolled down her limbs. She'd talked to herself too many times to be still dazzled by Patrick's charm, but the lecture hadn't worked.

"I accept your gift. Thanks." The memory of the smooth, rich taste triggered her longing to sneak another piece.

"But I'm the one who—"

"We're the ones, Christie. We both made mistakes. We're overly sensitive with each other."

"I know," she said, feeling overwhelmed by the mixture of emotions she dealt with daily.

"Let's make a pact."

She extended her hand. "The truth from now on."

He nodded, taking her fingers in his. "The truth, no matter how much it hurts. The truth and patience."

"Patience with each other." She felt his pulse against hers—life flowing through him. His life reviving her.

He squeezed her fingers and let go, eyeing his watch. "Sean will wonder where I am. I'd better find him."

Patrick smiled, spun around and vanished, leaving Christie faced with a loneliness when he walked away. She ambled across the room with her box of chocolates, touched by his willingness to forgive so easily.

"Chwistie?"

Sean's piping voice drew her around. She looked

at the miniature image of Patrick and moved toward him.

"Are you ready to go home?" she asked.

He shook his head no so hard Christie feared he'd get dizzy.

She knelt beside him. "Where are you going then?"

"On the pumpkin twain."

"The pumpkin train?"

"Not today, Sean," Patrick said. "This weekend."

Christie tousled the child's hair and gave Patrick a grin. "You can't mention events until you're walking out the door."

"Chwistie can come, too, Daddy." The boy's pleading face tilted upward to his father's.

Christie saw it coming and wondered if they needed time to get comfortable again. "I don't think I can—"

"Sure. Christie can come."

Their answers hit the air simultaneously.

"Goody." Sean clapped his hands, only hearing his father's response. He gave Christie a huge grin.

"But I wonder…" Her gaze lifted from Sean's to Patrick's.

"Sean asked you, Christie, and I'd love you to come along."

She looked at the child's eager expression. "Why not? I'll be Sean's date."

The boy grinned at her as if he understood about having a date.

"I don't mind playing second fiddle," Patrick said. "Better than no fiddle at all."

Patrick looked out the train window, watching the autumn colors flickering past. The northern air was brisk, but the train felt comfortable, and the soothing rhythm of the coach swaying like a cradle had rocked Sean to sleep, nestled in the seat beside him. The boy had been worn out with excitement, anticipating the visit of the Great Pumpkin who'd been on board the pumpkin train to greet the children. At the end of the ride, Sean would select his own pumpkin to take home.

But now silence settled over Patrick, and he eyed Christie in the seat facing his, her own eyes heavy as if the undulating motion had woven its charm on her, too.

She lifted her heavy lids and caught him watching her. "What are you looking at?"

"You...sleeping."

"I'm not sleeping. I'm resting my eyes."

He grinned at her excuse. The sunlight shimmered through the window, sending gold highlights through her hair and brightening her fair complexion. She'd worn a rust-colored sweater and beige slacks. In her dark green jacket, she seemed like autumn personified, all golden and burnished.

"Have you talked with your mother lately?" Patrick asked.

"My mother?" She frowned and leaned closer. "Not in the past few days. Why?"

"She dropped by to see my dad and brought over a casserole."

"Really?"

He saw concern settle on her face. "I'm surprised."

"Your mother's a nice lady. Why are you surprised?"

Christie shook her head and didn't answer.

"Because she was angry at me?" Patrick asked.

She shrugged, then gave him a puzzled look. "Did you tell her about—"

"No. That's between you and me."

She turned her head a moment and looked out the window. "I feel so badly about everything," she murmured, then turned to face him. "Both sides of the problem."

He captured her hand in his. "Christie, we've made a pact. Honesty and patience. We learned some valuable lessons about what we did and why it happened. We both had needs that we didn't address. Things we might have done to make things better for each other. But those are 'should haves,' and they're behind us. We have to move forward. Could we do that?"

"I'd like to put it behind me. Really." She hesitated, her nervousness evident in her downcast eyes.

"But first I want to ask if you can really forgive me."

Christie clung to his hand, and he felt the depth of her question. "I have forgiven you. The question is can you deal with all that's happened?"

She closed her eyes and nodded. "I think I can."

"Then let's focus on healing."

"I'd like that." She looked through the window again, the sunlight flickering through the trees against her profile. Finally she turned.

"Now, what's this about my mother?"

He chuckled at her abrupt shift in conversation. "She's been skeptical about our friendship. Worried about me hurting you again."

Christie nodded.

"I don't want to do that, Christie. Never. I've given our relationship a lot of thought. If this is what we can share, a day on the pumpkin train, that's all I'll ask for."

A questioning look filled her eyes. "You think you can live with that?"

He wanted to say "for now," but he didn't. "If I have to. Yes."

She seemed to think about what he'd said while her gaze drifted again to the view out the window. Finally she shifted closer. "Being honest, neither of us knows where this is going. Only time will tell, but I'll confess I miss you when you're not around. I never thought that would happen. But it has."

"I miss you, too. Sean misses you."

Her face twitched with concern, and she pulled back. "That's what I fear. I don't want Sean to get too attached to me in case things don't work out. He needs a mother, a woman he can count on."

Patrick watched her face darken. He agreed Sean's life would be easier with a mother, but that meant he needed a wife. He'd married twice. He'd loved them both in different ways, but Christie, she'd been the first and he couldn't forget what they might have had if they hadn't messed things up so badly. At times, he wondered if Christie were correct. Could they ever trust each other enough to contemplate marriage again? Could they accept the past and build a new life together?

"I've been struggling with something else, Patrick. Sometimes I fear that getting too attached to Sean is allowing him to be a surrogate to the child I've always wanted." She lowered her head. "I don't want to do that. I want to love him for himself. And then I have another worry."

Patrick's chest tightened as he watched the apprehension grow on her face.

"My mother said it a while back, something that's needled me every time I get comfortable with you."

"What is it?"

She bit the edge of her lip and looked at the floor before she finally lifted her head. "She said now that you're alone again, and with a child, you're probably just looking for someone to step in and—"

"Don't say that," Patrick said. "Your mother doesn't believe that anymore. She looks at it differently now. Talk with her. She thinks all of this has happened for a purpose."

"A purpose?" Her face lit with surprise. "Only my mother could come up with that."

He leaned forward and caught her hand in his. "Ask her." He released her fingers, realizing he was getting too close. Control. He had to overpower his emotions. "Christie, I'll make a promise. No more kisses. No more intimate gestures. Nothing but friendship. The kind we had when we first met. Remember those days? We were curious. Interested. But controlled. We had fun and enjoyed each other's company. If things change, we'll talk about it like adults."

"What about Sean?" Christie asked.

"He's young. I'm a stronger father than my dad was. And most important, I have God on my side. Sean will be okay with me." He said the words, but he recalled his occasional insecurity at being a father. Times when he wished he had a woman's advice. A gentle touch. A mother for Sean. But they'd survive, if they had to.

"I keep asking myself what makes us think we can work out our problems this time. We had good intentions when we first married, but we both failed. I wish I was certain this time could be forever, Patrick. I'm struggling with following my reason and following my heart."

''Follow your heart, Christie,'' he said.

She gave him a nod, and he saw her face relax.

Maybe they could work things out. She would be a friend he could count on and respect. A friend he could love without all the trappings of romance.

He glanced out the window and saw the scattered buildings of the town drawing closer. Soon Sean would be selecting a pumpkin.

Patrick wished that were the biggest choice he had to make. He'd made a promise to Christie, and no matter how badly he wanted things to be different, he would do what he could to keep his promise.

Chapter Thirteen

Hearing the hymn introduction, Christie opened her songbook and rose from the pew. She stood beside her parents and felt a deep sense of family commitment. She had learned a great deal in these past weeks, mainly that her anger all these years had been at herself and not at her parents or the church. Her mother had beamed when she'd arrived for the worship service. Christie knew her mother was thrilled that she'd come to church the last two Sundays.

The knowledge warmed Christie. She'd begun to understand the workings of the Lord. Things happened to help her grow in Him, to draw her closer, not push her away. But she needed to trust and have faith.

Last Sunday Christie had felt as if the lessons had

been for her. The words of Romans 5 rose in her thoughts throughout the week. *We also rejoice in our sufferings, because we know that suffering produces perseverance; perseverance, character; and character, hope. And hope does not disappoint us, because God has poured out his love into our hearts by the Holy Spirit, whom he has given us.*

Trust and hope. She'd needed both badly. Patrick had asked for friendship, but she hadn't trusted him. Truly, she hadn't trusted herself. The visions of the good days assailed her thoughts, luring her forward, making her hope for more. But Christie had realized last week that she had to hope in the Lord, not in herself. God would provide. She had suffered, and now she would persevere. She would hope and pray for God's direction.

First she wanted to tell Patrick he'd been correct about her expansion idea. Though she'd jumped on him about his comments regarding her addition, he'd been right. In the past weeks, she'd lost two students who'd been enrolled in a new child-care center closer to their homes. Patrick's words had rankled her, but they had been wise.

She'd enjoyed the pumpkin train. The conversation she and Patrick had shared had been honest. They'd opened their hearts, made an agreement that she hoped to keep.

When the service ended, Christie slid her hymn book into the pew rack and let her gaze drift. She spotted Patrick looking her way. He smiled and lifted Sean into his arms before he made his way to her.

Christie waved and sent him an accepting smile.

"You want to come by for dinner today?" Emma asked Christie, then turned, seeing Patrick walk up beside them.

"I can't, Mom," Christie said. "I promised Annie I'd drop by to see the new baby."

"That's so nice," Emma said. "I'm sure she's thrilled. Is Patrick going with you?"

Christie caught Patrick's puzzled look. "Mother's talking about Annie's new baby."

"Annie from Loving Care?" he asked.

Christie nodded. "They adopted."

"I'd love to go along, but I have Sean. He'd get in the way—"

"Sean wouldn't get in the way. Will you?" Emma asked resting her hand on the boy's shoulder. "But Sean might prefer to come to my house and play with the toy box."

"Toy box? At your house?" Christie asked, startled that her mother would offer, and even more startled that she had a toy box.

"It's in the hall closet," Emma said. "I always kept toys around for friends' children. For any child, for that matter, who might enter our lives." She gave Christie a pointed look.

Christie realized she'd not given her parents their only chance to have a grandchild. Though her mother didn't mean to hurt her, the truth filled Christie with disappointment and sadness. She would love to have a child, and she still might if she looked into adoption. The idea had possibilities.

Patrick looked surprised at Emma's offer, too. "I couldn't ask you to—"

"You didn't ask. I offered. I'd love to have Sean come for a visit." She knelt beside the boy. "Want to come and play with the toys, Sean? I have cookies."

The cookies piqued Sean's interest. He took Emma's hand without a qualm.

"After the visit, why don't you both come back for dinner?" Emma asked.

"Thanks," Patrick said, "but only if my dad's up to staying alone."

"We can fix him a plate. Better than eating carryout," she said, her smile broadening.

Patrick couldn't argue with that. He was startled at Emma's openness, as if she were welcoming him back into the family's life. "That would be nice. I'll give Dad a call."

With things settled, Patrick called his father, then headed for Annie's house on Washington Street with Christie leading the way. He'd met Annie at Loving Care and liked her right off. She had a way of opening her arms and her heart at the same time.

He parked at the curb and hurried around to open Christie's door. A suspicious look creased her forehead as if asking why he was being a gentleman.

She'd be surprised how much he'd changed over the years if she'd give him a chance to show her.

They headed up the walk and took the steps to a wide front porch with wicker furniture and an old-fashioned porch swing swaying with the cold November wind that whipped around the house. Patrick pulled his collar up around his neck as they waited for someone to answer the door.

Annie appeared and greeted them with a warm welcome.

They hurried inside and stepped from the small foyer into the living room. A portable crib sat beside a chair and Christie hurried there, bending over the opening, her voice reflecting her pleasure.

"She's beautiful," Christie whispered.

Patrick moved closer and agreed. The rosy-cheeked child had a cherub face with bowed lips, eyes closed, with long lashes resting against her ivory skin. "She's a keeper," Patrick said and stepped back to allow Annie room beside Christie.

He watched Christie's delight at seeing the little one-year-old, and his chest tightened as he remembered his part in stopping them from having a child of their own. Now he delighted in his son and Annie had a daughter, while Christie had no one. If he could only do it over again. But those were wishes and dreams, not reality.

"Have a seat," Annie said. "Ken should be back soon. He ran to the store for me."

"What did you name her, Annie?"

"I wanted a name that meant blessing. We called her Gracelynne."

"What a pretty name."

"I found it on the Internet. It's perfect."

Christie nodded, and Patrick saw deep longing reflected in her face for the same kind of blessing.

When Annie waved them toward the chairs again, Christie settled on the sofa. Patrick sat beside her and listened as the talk drifted from babies to Loving Care and all its happenings since Annie had taken her short leave to welcome the child to her home.

"I'm a rotten hostess," Annie said, leaping from the chair. "I made fresh coffee and forgot."

Christie halted her with a gesture. "We're not staying long, so please—"

"You have time for coffee," she said, hurrying from the room.

The sound of her voice must have wakened the toddler. In seconds the child's wiggling caught Christie's attention, and she bounded from the sofa to the crib. "Hi, there," she said. "Welcome to Annie's world, Gracelynne."

Patrick marveled at the vision, watching Christie lift the child in her arms and nestle her against her cheek. Christie was meant to be a mother. He'd seen her at Loving Care—her gentleness, her concern and love for the children.

The picture wrapped him in sadness and guilt. Though he could do nothing about the past, the thought whetted his longing to make a difference in her future. To let love happen again the way it was meant to. But they needed time and he needed to control himself.

Annie returned, and Christie let her coffee cool while she cuddled the little girl in her arms. He remembered her singing lullabies to Sean, and his sorrow deepened. *Dear Lord, you can work miracles. Let Christie see me with new eyes if it's Your will.* He sent the prayer heavenward, hoping that the Lord's will and his were on the same wavelength.

Looking through the car window, Christie's senses still clung to the child she'd held in her arms—the soft, pink flesh, the scent of talcum, the warmth and love that nestled against her chest. Even Patrick had held the child, his large hands supporting the little girl against his broad chest, her smiles and his sparkling eyes. He looked at ease, not like many men who shied away from little ones. The vision covered her with melancholy.

"You're thinking," Patrick said, breaking through her reverie.

"Thinking about Annie and Ken and Gracelynne."

"It's a blessing. That little girl will be loved by two great people."

His words settled uneasily in her chest. "I'm not trying to drag up old issues, but I wonder if I would have been a good mother. I like to think so."

"How can you question that, Christie? You're a

natural.'' His hand slid across the empty space and pressed her arm. ''I enjoyed seeing the baby, but it made me sad, guilty really. I'll never forgive myself for asking you to wait before having our child. I was so wrong.''

''Maybe not, at least not in our situation. A divorce is consuming. I was so filled with anger and hurt. If I'd had a child, he or she would have sensed my bitterness, felt it and the bad feelings would have made an impression. Whether I like it or not, maybe God knows what He's doing.''

Her ridiculous comment made her laugh, and Patrick joined her. The sound of their lighthearted chuckle filled the car and edged out the gloom and longing she'd been feeling.

''It's nice to hear you laugh,'' Patrick said. ''I've missed that.''

''Me, too,'' she said, remembering nights so long ago when they'd spent time laughing, even climbing into bed and recalling humorous things that had happened during the day. They'd often laughed themselves to sleep. Where had those fun-filled days gone?

''I could adopt,'' Christie said, letting the words escape before she'd locked the door on her thoughts. She startled herself with the admission and glanced at Patrick to see his reaction.

He didn't move, but kept his eyes on the highway, but she could almost hear the gears cranking in his thoughts. Then she noticed his jaw tighten and his full lips draw into a straight line.

"Why would you think to adopt now?" he asked. "You're still young enough to have children."

"You've forgotten. Besides my age, my condition is worse now. Endometriosis doesn't get better. It only heightens and makes conception impossible. Anyway, I'm not married and don't plan to be." Saying the words aloud to Patrick broke her heart. Her imagination played with her mind, conjuring up romantic moments with him again, like the brief kiss they'd shared.

"It's my fault and there's nothing I can do," Patrick said. "I wish there were."

If wishes were horses, Christie's mind rattled out the old saying, but beneath her skepticism, she realized he could do something. She could do something. They could marry again, if only... The "if only" halted her thoughts. She'd created the "if onlys" and she was the only one who could make them go away.

Patrick pulled away from the hardware store heading for Loving Care to pick up Sean. When he'd spoken to Christie earlier, she'd mentioned wanting to talk with him if he had time. Time. He had all the time in the world. But now, she'd aroused his curiosity.

A fine mist of snowflakes drifted past the windshield, leaving moist dots on the pane. He turned on the wipers but the window only streaked, leaving a blurry view of the gray day. Since Christie's call, his spirit felt drab.

What had happened to his optimism? He'd clung to a distant hope that one day all would be well between them. Yet each time they spoke, he waited for the guillotine to drop. He'd asked himself why he persisted, and the answer seemed easy. Because he'd fallen in love with Christie again, and this time he was confident they could make it work.

He pushed the lever for the window washer and the view brightened. For a moment the clouds parted and a hazy sun spread its rays on the cold earth. He grasped at the hidden promise that beneath the clouds and haze he'd see a golden sun again.

Loving Care came into view, and his stomach knotted. He wondered what Christie wanted to talk about. He sent a quick prayer to the Lord for wisdom and fortitude. He needed both badly.

Outside the November wind flapped the tail of his fleece-lined jacket, and he shoved his hands into his pockets as he hurried up the center's sidewalk. He waited only a moment for Bev to open the door and send him a warm greeting.

The comfortable temperature inside the room welcomed him as well, and without hesitation, he strode toward Christie's office, hoping the welcome and warmth were signs of what was to come.

''Hi,'' Christie said, seeing him at the doorway.

She beckoned him inside. "I'm glad you didn't have plans. I really need to talk with you."

Her face looked calm and her stance relaxed, giving Patrick hope. "No problem. What's up?" he asked, trying to sound upbeat and assured.

She motioned him toward a chair near her desk, and he stepped forward with a mix of emotion.

"Actually," she said, coming around the desk and leaning against the corner. "I want to apologize."

"Apologize?" He tried to stop the frown that appeared on his face. "About what?"

"What you said about the addition. I jumped on you because I felt threatened and belittled. I don't know what I felt, but you suggested I wait on making any big plans, and I said you were interfering."

"I was. I admitted that. This is your business, and you've done a bang-up job without my two cents worth."

She shook her head. "But you were right." Within a few moments, she'd explained about the other child-care center opening in town and her loss of enrollment.

Instead of feeling smug, Patrick felt disappointed. "I wish it hadn't happened, Christie. You had some nice ideas there. I'd have been thrilled for you to see the place grow and prove me wrong. I don't know why I opened my mouth that day. Habit, I guess."

"You did me a favor. The only loss I really feel

is a room for keeping sick kids away from the others. It's a real problem when a child gets here and we realize he has measles or a virus. It spreads so easily. By the time the child's parents arrive, the germs have spread to the others."

Patrick gave her concern some thought. "You might have room somewhere else you could spare. A cot in a quiet spot wouldn't take too much space." He swung his hand across the room. "Even that corner by the window. You could put a cot there and block it with one of those screens. It's only temporary."

Christie's face brightened as she pushed away from the desktop and strode across the room. She held her chin between her thumb and finger, studying the space for a moment. "You know, that might work. I could pull that copy machine away from the wall and put it against a screen, leaving space behind."

"It should work," he said, pleased that she'd accepted his opinion without balking. "The waiting room might work, too."

"I like having spillover space for the kids to play. Right here would work well. Thanks for the idea." She walked to him and wrapped her arms around his neck, giving him a hug.

Her action surprised, yet pleased him. So natural, so real, so accepting—it slid over him like a warm glove.

Christie eased back, but didn't move far. The

closeness seemed right, and Patrick rested his hand on her shoulder.

"How's your dad?" Christie asked.

"Doing well."

"I should stop by?"

"He'd love that. How about tonight? I promised him a home-cooked meal…and I could use some help."

"Are you inviting me or my cooking skills?"

"You first. The skills are a bonus."

She grinned. "Then I'll accept."

Her ready agreement felt like a gift, and Patrick's mind flew with plans. He needed groceries. "I'd better get Sean and head to the grocery store or we'll eat at midnight."

"I'll bring Sean home. You go ahead."

"Really?"

"Sure. Why not?"

His spirit lifted. He gave Christie a hug and dashed toward the door, realizing she'd hugged him back.

Chapter Fourteen

Christie stood at Patrick's sink, running hot water over the dishes before placing them into the dishwasher.

"You don't have to do that," Patrick said, leaning beside her clutching a dishcloth in his hand.

"You do your job, and I'll do mine. You're wiping up the stove."

He chuckled and moved away, whistling as he always did as he worked. She heard him clanging burners as he removed the spatters from the stove. They'd made spaghetti and meatballs—the quick version. But it had been delicious, and Christie had gotten a kick out of watching Sean eat the noodles.

The evening had taken her back, and only once in a while did she feel a twinge of regret or envy when she focused on Sean's peaked chin, reminding her of the woman who gave him birth. If she centered her attention on his eyes and nose, the child was all Patrick.

"I think I'll put Sean to bed," Patrick said, as he draped the dishcloth on the edge of the sink. "Dad's in the living room shuffling cards. I'm sure he'd love a game of hearts. He always wins."

"I haven't played hearts since…" She didn't finish. She didn't have to. Patrick would remember the evenings they'd gotten together with friends and had the big hearts challenge.

Christie stood in the kitchen alone, thinking back to times they'd come to visit their folks. They tried to split the visit between Patrick's father and her parents, even spending the night in the bedroom upstairs—Patrick's old bed—a double where they were nestled like spoons, fingers woven together, body pressed to body—secure and comfortable. The memory kicked her heart to a gallop until she slammed the door on the unwanted nostalgia.

When she stepped into the living room, she knew Patrick was correct. Joe leaned back in his recliner, a deck of playing cards fluttering in a shuffle.

"Tired?" she asked, already knowing the answer to the question.

"No. I'm feeling good tonight," he said, his eyes telling her why he felt so well.

"Looks like you're up for a game of solitaire." She grinned, goading him on.

"No. Hearts, but I need a couple of players."

"I wonder who those might be." Patrick's voice sailed from the doorway. He came into the room and clamped his hand on his father's shoulders. "Do you want me to bring in a card table?"

"Can't play on the air," Joe said, his chuckle brightening his gaunt face.

In minutes, Christie found herself on one side of a card table, playing a game she knew she would lose, but the activity bound them in laughter and chatter as they slapped a heart onto the play…or worse, the queen of spades, adding points to the score—points they didn't want since the low score won.

When she reached one hundred, Patrick and his father cackled as she was crowned loser. Joe had won by three points, and made his way to bed with confidence that, even with a bad heart, he could at least play the game of hearts like a champ.

As Patrick put the card table away, Christie gathered her jacket and shoulder bag, ready to leave.

"You're not leaving?" Patrick said, coming into the living room and eyeing the coat on her arm.

His face took on his boyish pleading that sent Christie's heart on a wild ride.

"You don't have to leave, do you?" he asked.

She glanced at her watch. "It's getting late."

"Stay for a while longer."

She felt the grin curve her mouth and knew she'd given in. "Just for a minute. Then I'm out of here."

He motioned her toward the sofa. "It's been a nice evening. I hate it to end."

"It has."

She followed his gesture and sank onto the cushion. "It's good seeing your dad a little more chipper."

"I think it's when you're around."

"Blarney," she said, pushing his words away with her gesture.

"No. I mean it. It's like a healing. He told me how bad he felt when you'd avoided each other. I know why it happened, but I'm glad it's over."

"Me, too." Her mother's changed attitude came to mind. "By the way, Mom's invited all of you for Thanksgiving dinner."

"Really?" Patrick's eyebrows lifted over his questioning eyes.

"It's been hard for her, and I know she still has reservations about our relationship. She's worried that I'll get tangled up with you again, hurt again, but I told her not to worry." Christie realized the statement left a multiple of interpretations, meanings she'd just begun to deal with herself.

Patrick's gaze searched hers. "How do you feel about the invitation?"

"Thanksgiving's a day to share. Even the pilgrims and Indians got together. Remember?"

He shrugged. "Interesting way to look at it."

Christie was sorry she'd used that example. It connoted strangers. People from different worlds together for a moment, but not a lifetime. Weariness washed over her. She'd struggled too long with the issues surrounding her relationship with Patrick. Christie needed some sign to let her know that love could happen and be forever. She wanted to be assured that she could forget Sean's parentage—as Patrick had said before—and that she could open her arms and love the child fully for who he was. She longed for God's direction, but hadn't felt it yet. Maybe she'd waited too long to ask the Lord for guidance, or maybe God had already spoken and she'd missed His message.

"What should I tell my mother?" Christie asked finally, turning to the present.

Patrick sat in thought as she had done. His head drooped over his folded hands resting between his knees. He raised his head. "It's up to Dad. I'll have to let you know if that's okay. Tell your mom we appreciate the invitation."

Christie sensed their conversation losing its spontaneity, as if they'd begun to tiptoe again, afraid of what they might say. But seeing his face filled her with a warmth that gave her courage to be honest…to take a risk. "It's been a long time since we've celebrated Thanksgiving together. I really hope you can come."

He raised his eyes to hers and in them she saw such deep feeling it took her breath away.

"I do, too," he said.

* * *

"You're sure, Dad?"

"I'd be a fool to go out in this weather," Joe said, staring out the front window at the heavy snow that had fallen overnight and stood in deep mounds over everything in sight.

"I shoveled the driveway and walk, and I'll warm the car for you," Patrick said, hating to leave his father home alone on Thanksgiving.

"Emma and Wes will understand, and I know Emma will send me home enough food for a week."

Patrick grinned, knowing his father was right.

"And don't rush," Joe said. "I have some ham here and those scalloped potatoes you made from a box, but they weren't bad. I'll admit that. Just bring Emma's dinner home later tonight. I'll enjoy it tomorrow."

No sense in fighting city hall. He knew when his father had his mind set. Patrick zippered Sean's jacket and helped him tug on his boots, then grabbed his navy jacket and plaid scarf. He dug a pair of leather gloves from his pockets. "We're going then. If you need me, I wrote down the telephone number by the kitchen phone. Okay?"

"Okay. So get on your way, or you'll be late."

"They'll be disappointed you're not coming," Patrick said, giving one last try at changing his mind.

His father's look was all he needed for a response.

"I'll call you later," Patrick said, hoisting Sean in his arms and heading to his car.

The wind had died down, but a crisp feeling hung in the air. Sunshine peeked from behind a cloud, creating diamonds in the pristine snow. Sean eyed the fluff with amazement, as if he'd never seen a snowfall. "Snow," he said, then held his tongue out to catch a flake.

Patrick settled him into the car seat, then climbed in and backed down the driveway.

The roads were clear but slick, and he eased his way around the last corner, happy to see the Goodson house. He parked in the driveway behind Christie's sedan, and climbed out. While he leaned over the back seat to loosen Sean from the belts, a thud whacked him in the behind.

He swung around to find Christie bundled up in a scarf and down jacket near the porch. She'd bent over to form another snowball, and seeing her gleeful smile, Patrick grabbed Sean in his arms while he called to her over his shoulder. "I have a hostage."

Her laugh tickled him, and when he faced her, he held Sean in front of him. Sean wiggled to get down, curious about the snow. Patrick lowered him to the ground, and stealthily scooped up a handful of white stuff, squeezing it into a ball, then fired it at Christie.

She ducked, but the glob hit her hair. She brushed it away and came toward him, laughing. "I surrender," she said.

He checked her hands to make sure they were

empty. She wore mittens matted with pea-size lumps of crystalized snow.

"Let's make a snowman for Sean," she said, bending down to form a ball.

He eyed her action, making sure it wasn't a trick. When he saw she was serious, he closed the distance. "What about dinner? Shouldn't we be helping your mother?"

"Everything's under control. We're just waiting another forty minutes for the turkey to be ready."

Hearing that, Patrick joined her, helping Sean to roll a smaller ball to make the snowman's head. His fingers became frigid as the snow dampened his gloves, but he didn't want to let go of the joy he felt, spending time with Sean and Christie making a snowman.

The snow glimmered like his heart sparkling with a renewed joy. They worked together, lifting the large spheres, one on top of the other. Christie's cheeks glowed and her nose reddened with the cold while she scrounged beneath the large tree to find two sticks for arms. He and Shawn had found a few pebbles in the flower beds hidden beneath the mounds, and he let Sean plop them into the snowman's face to form its features.

Finished, they stood back, he and Christie arm in arm with Sean in his other, admiring their amateur creation.

A rap at the window signaled them, and they headed up the porch steps. Patrick knocked the snow from his shoes onto the mat before stepping into the warmth inside, knowing the furnace could never radiate the kind of heat that already burned in his heart.

Later as they sat around the table enjoying the end of the meal, Patrick's thoughts drifted to the snowman and the perfect pleasure he'd shared with Christie. In the silence of his thoughts, he sent a thank-you to God for the day, for the healing he felt and for giving him hope of things to come.

"Patrick, how's your father doing?" Wes asked.

"Good. He didn't want to get out in the cold, but the doctor thinks he's doing great. He had an appointment a few days ago."

"Praise God," Emma said, her gentle face letting him know she really cared.

"I thought I'd lose him a while back, but it looks like he'll have more years if he takes care of himself. In fact, I'm thinking about looking for my own place soon."

"Really?" Christie said. "You didn't tell me."

Patrick smiled. "I was waiting for the right time. I wanted to con you into helping me find a house." He couldn't admit the real reason to her parents, not until he talked with her. Hope glowed like a jewel in his thoughts.

Emma rose and slid back her chair. "I'll make up a big plate for your dad," she said, reaching out to clear the table. "Enough for all of you, and I have an extra pie."

"Dad'll enjoy it, but don't overdo. Just a meal for him will be great." He checked his watch, noticing how time had flown. "I'd better call him if you don't mind. I'm still a watchdog. I want to make sure he's okay."

"Go ahead," Wes said. "Use the telephone in the living room. It's quieter there."

Patrick rose, still amazed to see Sean sitting on Wes's knee, his cheeks rosy from playing outside, his head leaning against Wes's broad chest. The two had stuck together like adhesive.

Christie watched Patrick leave the room. Her heart lifted at what they'd shared—normal, relaxed fun in the snow. She eyed her father holding Sean as if he were his grandchild. Though a jab of sadness made her recall her usual "what ifs," she'd grown fond of the child. If she were to admit the truth, she cared for the child more than she had dreamed possible. In her deep caring, she had let go of her anger and hurt—those feelings she'd lived with for so long.

The realization lightened her heart. She felt good letting go. Was this how it felt when she handed her burdens to the Lord? Could God's grace and mercy boost her spirit so completely? Uplift her and fill her with joy? Could this be what she'd been missing for so long?

Patrick came through the doorway all smiles.

"He's fine," he said, sinking back to the chair he'd vacated and eyeing Sean. "But either I need to get going or find a place to lay my boy, unless you want to hold him the rest of the evening.''

Her father chuckled. ''I think we can find a spot.'' He looked at Christie. ''Why not put him in the spare bedroom?''

She rose and waited for Patrick to lift Sean in his arms. She beckoned him forward, and he followed her to the only bedroom on the first floor—a small room, but one that worked well for company.

Patrick laid Sean on the bed, and Christie unfolded an afghan that had lain at the foot and covered the child. His rosy cheeks seemed brighter than earlier, and she smiled, remembering how much fun they'd had outside.

In the living room, the men gathered around the television watching the football game, and Christie and her mother chatted with half an eye on the plays. When the game ended, they enjoyed the pumpkin pie. Then afterward, her parents excused themselves, Christie was sure, to give Patrick and her time alone.

Their action surprised her. Months ago, Christie's mother had stood guard over her, concerned about her feelings and afraid of her involvement with Patrick. Today she sensed encouragement. The awareness left her thoughtful.

Patrick rose from the chair near the TV and plopped onto the sofa beside Christie.

''It's been a great day,'' he said. ''Like...'' His voice faded.

She shook her head. ''Let's focus on the present.''

He nodded, his face serious. "I know. Still, I can't help but wish that things had been different." He touched her arm, and she lifted her eyes to his. "Don't get me wrong," he said. "I cherish this time with you and your family. I'm so glad Sean has the opportunity to know your folks. It's just that…"

His voice faded again, and Christie finished his sentence in her head—it was hard to stop at friendship. "I know what you mean."

"Do you?"

"I think so."

He rested his palm against her hand. "We've shared our lives in such a personal and intimate way. Sure we had bad times. I've talked them through until I'm weary, but I remember the good times, too. The times that were special."

"Perfect times," she said, feeling a deep yearning to say something she'd never said before. She drew in a deep breath. "Losing you was horrible. It hurt my pride and it hurt me. I felt lonely and empty, but I also felt deep anger." She turned to face him squarely. "You know why?"

He shrugged. "For all the things you said, I suppose. I ruined your life."

"You ruined my *perfect* life. *Perfect* is the key. You know how important it has always been to me to have everything orderly, to give the best party, to keep my home the neatest. Perfection. I'll accept nothing less."

"And that's why we have no chance to be more

than we are," he said, his voice darkening with awareness.

"Not really. I've changed a little in the past months."

His downcast gaze swung upward, a glimmer of hope reflected in his eyes. "Changed?"

"I'm still a nitpicker, I suppose, but I realize that in the Lord all things are perfected. So when things aren't humanly perfect, we can give them to God who'll make them better. Does that make sense?"

"Perfect sense."

Hearing the word *perfect* again caused her to grin, and it felt good. "I've learned a perfect marriage is unrealistic. Anything takes work. Like my business. I try to do my best, but things happen—things outside my control. And I've learned not to give up, not to shut the door, but to open it wider and face the problem. I've changed that much."

"Both of us have learned things. Keeping feelings inside gets me nowhere. How can I heal if I keep my problems and fears inside to fester and swell until the molehill has become the mountain. Knowing God has helped with that."

"You've been honest with me, Patrick. I know we were both wrong."

He reached for her hand, and clasped it in his. "Let's look to the future," he said, his face bright with hope. His expression was as warm and gentle as a spring breeze.

"We're back to a solid friendship," he said. "I

can handle that for now. If God wills, He'll direct us into something deeper. That's what I've been praying for.''

"I've been praying, too. I care so much about you, but when I think of us going beyond the way we are today, I worry. Could we slip back into our old habits? Could the mistakes we made once have caused too much damage? Can we ever really trust each other again?'' She felt tears pool in her eyes. "And Sean. Even though he's a sweet child, will I ever stop thinking about Sherry when I look at him?''

"He's my son, Christie. Think of me. Think of us. Think of the children we still could have, endometriosis or not. God's in charge.''

Patrick was right. God was in charge. Yet knowing that and accepting it were two different things. Since rebuilding her friendship with Patrick, the fear of losing him again had heightened. She didn't want to return to her empty, lonely life. Instead, she needed to cling to the happiness she felt today, knowing she and Patrick were both in the hands of a caring and loving Lord.

He touched her hand. "I've told you Sean and I can get by alone, but a mother is important, Christie. Sean needs a mother really, and that person could be you.''

Sean needs a mother. The words punched her in the solar plexus. Was this all about Sean needing a mother? Patrick didn't love her, but he felt so comfortable with her that he figured she'd be as good as anyone to be a mother to Sean. Was that it? Her heart ached at the thought.

A whimper struck them at the same time. Patrick released her hands and was gone before she moved. His abruptness sent her reeling, but hearing Sean's cry and rasping cough, she rose and followed Patrick to the bedroom. When she came through the doorway, a new concern filled her thoughts.

Sean's cheeks were fiery red, and beads of perspiration budded on his nose. She stood beside Patrick, running her hand across the child's face and feeling the heat.

"He has a fever," she said.

"I noticed he hasn't been himself for the past couple of days. I shouldn't have let him play outside. I could kick myself."

She grasped his arm. "Playing outside wouldn't hurt him. You had him bundled up well. This must be a virus or something. I'll see if Mom has some baby aspirins." She moved toward the doorway and stopped. "If she has a toy box, she should have some children's aspirin, I'd hope." She tried to lighten the tension she was feeling, but it didn't work. Confusion and worry still knotted her muscles, and strain sullied Patrick's handsome face.

In moments, Emma had joined them, hovering over the child, wiping his face with a cool cloth and checking his temperature.

"It's one hundred and two," she said shaking

down the thermometer. "Kids often have fevers. Just keep an eye on him, but don't let the temperature get much higher before calling the doctor."

"I'd better get him home," Patrick said, "before it gets colder outside.

Emma gave Sean a baby aspirin, then found a heavy blanket to protect him from the cold.

Patrick wrapped Sean like a cocoon, then lifted him into his arms.

"Now you keep us posted, Patrick," Emma said.

"Should I ride with you?" Christie asked, following him to the doorway, forgetting her upset with what he'd said earlier. Now, she was frightened not by Sean's fever, but his tight cough and rattling breathing.

"No. It's not far, and then how would you get back?"

"I could follow you in my car," she said.

"It's still cold and slippery. I'll call you after you get home. Sean's had a fever before. This one just surprised me."

Emma waited by the doorway, too, tucking the blanket around Sean's ears until only his nose peeked out, but Christie couldn't rid herself of the picture of Sean's listlessness and his bright red cheeks.

She watched Patrick leave, her thoughts spiraling out of control. She'd settle her upset with Patrick later. Now the child's illness triggered deepest concern.

Awareness charged through her. No, Sean wasn't her child, and he never would be where blood was concerned. He belonged to Sherry and Patrick, but if she didn't love the boy as her own, why did she feel such anxiety? Such profound concern?

Chapter Fifteen

Christie couldn't sleep after learning Sean's fever
had risen a degree when he'd gotten home. Although
Patrick promised to call if anything else happened,
that didn't help. Waiting and wondering, Christie
watched the clock moving slowly, like a dirge.

After tossing and turning for hours, she rose and
slipped into jeans and a holiday sweatshirt adorned
with a choir of angels hovering in a blue sky. Hard
to believe, but Christmas was only weeks away.

She filled the coffeemaker and sat at the table,
staring at the telephone. Five o'clock. She hoped
Patrick was sleeping, knowing Sean was feeling better. But she wasn't. Alien sensations filled her
mind—her feelings for Sean and the conversation
she'd had with Patrick.

At first, she'd felt good about their honest discussion, but Patrick's final statement had thrown her off balance. He'd insinuated he wanted to remarry her. To try again. *Think of the children we still could have,* he'd said. What else could that mean? But in the next breath, he'd let her know he wanted a mother for Sean. What did Patrick want? Did he really love her, or was she a familiar convenience?

She'd begun to think he'd fallen in love with her once more, as she had with him. Yes, she'd been afraid to admit it openly, but the feelings were there, poking her like a nail in her shoe. She'd nearly allowed herself to trust him. One minute their relationship seemed so right. The next, so wrong. Deep hurt pushed against her chest and constricted her breathing.

Christie pressed her face in her hands and prayed. *Lord, I know You said we should rejoice in our sufferings, because suffering produces hope. But my hope has faded, and I can't sort reality from dreams. I need to trust again. Help me to see clearly. Let me know Your will.*

The clock hands inched around the dial. Five-thirty. Five-fifty. Christie wavered between disappointment and worry. At six she could stand it no longer. She rose and headed for the phone. Its ring just as she reached it sent her heart to her throat.

"Patrick?" she said into the receiver.

"Did I wake you?"

"Are you kidding? I've been awake all night."

"So have I. I just called and got the doctor's answering service. Now I'm waiting for him to call back."

She closed her eyes in frustration. "How long? Did she say?"

"I don't know. It's a holiday weekend. He's not in the office until Monday."

Christie's heart sank. "I can't sit here any longer. I'm coming over. I'll be there in a few minutes."

Before he could argue, Christie hung up and grabbed her jacket, figuring she'd be there before the doctor returned Patrick's call.

Patrick put down the receiver and stared at the telephone, waiting. The two people he loved most filled his thoughts—his son and Christie. He'd sensed a problem last night when Christie had suddenly withdrawn. He'd reviewed their conversation and couldn't understand what had triggered the change.

But he couldn't concentrate on that now. Christie was on her way. She'd offered to come last night for that matter. His mind whirred with confusion. He couldn't deal with any of it now. Maybe Sean's fever was only one of those childhood scares. He knew they happened, but until he knew for sure what it was, he'd never rest.

Patrick had so hoped he and Christie could find a way to mend their wounds and grow together again. Benjamin Franklin's adage remembered from high school leaped into his thoughts. *A cracked plate never mends.* Was that true for them? No. He and Christie weren't a cracked plate. They were two people who had loved and let fears push them apart until they could no longer see each other but only feel the deep abyss between them. He'd thought they'd begun to build a bridge, a sturdy bridge to bring them back together, but something had removed a spike from the span. Once again they stood on shaky ground. Would it ever change?

The telephone's ring sent his pulse on a sprint, and he grasped the receiver, feeling relief when he heard the doctor's voice asking about Sean.

"His temperature is nearly one hundred and five, and I've given him children's ibuprofen as often as it's allowed, but it's not dropping."

"Any other symptoms?" the doctor asked.

"A tight cough, raspy breathing, and he started vomiting this morning."

The line hung with silence, and Patrick clung to the telephone, his palms moist. "What do you think?" he asked, unable to wait for the doctor's response.

"We'd better not take any chances," the man said. "Take him to emergency. I'll call to let them know you're on your way."

"Emergency?" Disappointment struck Patrick's heart. He'd preferred the doctor's office where Sean had been before, not an unfamiliar hospital to frighten him.

"If it's nothing serious, they'll send him back

home, and you can bring him in on Monday. If he's admitted, I'll see him there.''

Patrick stared at the mouthpiece, wondering about devotion to patients and concern for little children. Shouldn't a pediatric doctor be more caring? He pushed the thought aside. The physician received calls from frightened parents morning and night. The man deserved a day off.

When Patrick put down the receiver, he headed toward Sean's room, but before he made it, the doorbell rang. Christie stood on the threshold, her face pinched with alarm.

''Did you hear anything?'' she asked, stepping inside.

''He told me to take him to emergency.''

Without asking questions, she hurried past him, dropping her shoulder bag onto a nearby chair. ''What can I do?''

In moments, they had Sean ready to go while Patrick's father stood by, his face riddled with concern. Outside, Patrick climbed into his car after settling Christie in the back seat with Sean. Once strapped in, they were on their way.

The traffic was light early in the morning, and when they arrived, Patrick got out with Sean and let Christie park the car in the emergency area. She found them, her jacket smelling of winter air and her face mottled from the cold and, he knew, worry.

Patrick turned to follow as they swept Sean away on a gurney.

"I'll be in the waiting room," Christie said, backing toward the area.

He caught her arm. "No. Come with me."

She drew back, but he pulled her along, wanting her there for his own reasons. No matter what she said, he knew her feelings were strong for his son and he wouldn't allow her to wait alone at a time like this.

They entered the cubicle and stood aside while the orderly situated Sean. A nurse arrived, and when she took Sean's temperature, Patrick leaned forward trying to read the numbers she'd written, but the woman had covered them too quickly. Before he could ask, she whipped through the doorway.

Patrick pulled the lone chair toward Christie and gestured for her to sit. She sank into it while he stood over Sean, listening to his ragged breathing. Guilt filled him. What could he have done to keep his son safe?

Hearing the curtain slide back, Patrick turned as the physician entered.

"I'm Dr. Kedar," he said, extending his hand.

Patrick shook it, his own cold and trembling. "Dr. Minkin sent us here." He gestured helplessly. "My son—"

"Yes, I know. He said your boy has a high fever, difficulty breathing and has been vomiting since yesterday."

Patrick shook his head. "The vomiting started today."

"When did you notice the fever?" the doctor asked, pulling a stethoscope from his lab coat pocket and listening to Sean's lungs.

"After Thanksgiving dinner yesterday. We'd been playing in the snow earlier so I thought his rosy cheeks were from that. I should have known—"

Christie put his hand on her arm and shook her head. He heeded her warning. No sense dragging out "what ifs" and "should haves." The concern was for Sean, not his own ineptness as a father.

Sean's listless form looked limp and unaware as the doctor moved him up and back to listen to his breathing.

"What is it?" Patrick asked.

The physician gave him a cursory glance, continuing to check Sean's pulse and scrutinize Sean's nose and ears. He put the instruments back onto the tray before he answered. "I'll need a chest X-ray and a culture before I can be certain."

"Is it an infection?"

"The body uses fever to kill bacteria and viruses that cause infection...so yes, it's most probable he has an infection. The culture will help pinpoint what we're dealing with."

Patrick stood behind Christie and gripped the chair back. "Is this serious?"

"If the bacteria is meningococcus. Yes. Your son has the symptoms—high fever, difficulty breathing, and vomiting. Has he had painful joints or a stiff neck and back?''

''I don't think so. He didn't complain about that.'' Patrick studied the doctor's face, looking for a sign.

''That's good news. We'll know what it is soon.'' He moved toward the door. ''Someone will be in to do the culture, and then we'll take him to X-ray. We'll let you know when he's back.''

''Should we wait here?'' Patrick asked, hating to leave Sean in case he awakened.

''You can until they take him to X-ray.'' The doctor left, and Patrick moved to Sean's side.

Christie joined him, running her hands along the child's arm and petting his hairline where moisture beaded from the fever. ''I'd do anything to be here in his place.''

Patrick wrapped his arm around her shoulder. ''Me, too,'' he said, touched by her concern.

The curtain glided back, and an orderly stepped in. ''I need to move your son to X-ray.''

Patrick shifted aside, but Christie lingered, her hand on Sean's cheek.

''He'll be okay, Mom,'' the young man said, sliding in beside her.

Christie shifted, her mouth opening as if to explain his error. She moved aside without comment, an uneasy look on her face, and Patrick took her arm, guiding her away from the cubicle.

''The waiting room is to the left when you go through the double doors,'' the young man said.

Patrick placed his arm around her shoulder as they headed through the door. His mind juggled his thoughts— Christie's and his deep concern for Sean, but, as well, Christie's unintended admission. She loved Sean, whether she acknowledged it or not.

In the waiting room, the doctor's comment flew into his mind. He didn't like the sound. "Do you know anything about mengi-something-coccus, whatever the doctor said?"

Christie sat a moment and gnawed on the corner of her lip. "*Meninges* has to do with the brain. I think it's the tissue around it. Something like that."

"That doesn't sound good. I know *coccus* refers to bacteria, so that must mean—"

Christie grasped his arm and gave it a squeeze. "Please don't try to guess what it is, Patrick. You'll scare us both. Let's just wait until we hear from the doctor."

Patrick nodded, and though he didn't speak his concern, it weighed on his mind and heart. The possibility of Sean having a bacteria in the brain, like meningitis, frightened him.

Time dragged. Though he and Christie talked about other things, nothing they addressed seemed important to Patrick. The longer they waited, the more each tried to second guess what had happened. Christie blamed herself. She needed a quarantine room at the center. Patrick feared he'd let Sean play in the snow too long.

The conversation faded, and they sat in stony silence with their own thoughts. Patrick wanted to ask Christie about yesterday. Why she'd withdrawn and what he'd done to cause it. They seemed to walk on eggshells with each other, both afraid to do or say something that might cause stress between them. Only God could make a difference, and he'd prayed for the Lord's help daily.

When Dr. Kedar came through the doorway, Patrick shot from his chair like an arrow taut in the bow. He beckoned to Christie.

She rose but remained near her chair.

Patrick's chest tightened as he waited for the physician to speak.

"We won't have the culture results for a while yet, but the X-ray indicates it's probably not meningitis. From what we can tell now, your son has pneumonia."

The physician's words sent Patrick on a spiral of both relief and worry. "Pneumonia? That's serious."

"Better than meningitis," the doctor said. "Pneumonia is a good guess. What kind of infection we'll know later. I'm afraid he's already dehydrated from the vomiting and fever. You understand, he'll have to be admitted."

"Admitted, but…"

"He's better off here, Patrick," Christie said, stepping to his side and wrapping her hand around his forearm. "Even though it's difficult."

"Your wife is right," the man said. "We'll start

him on antibiotics. Does he have allergies to penicillin?''

''Not that I know of,'' Patrick said.

''Good. We'll start with that. He'll be feeling better as soon as we begin treatment.''

Christie gestured toward the waiting-room doorway. ''Can we—''

''Certainly,'' the doctor said, not waiting for her to finish. ''He's back in the same cubicle. We'll have him in a room shortly.''

Patrick eyed Christie, amazed that she'd never flinched when the doctor had called her his wife. Her only focus was Sean. He sent God a thank-you for the amazing turn of events.

''I keep picturing Sean looking so helpless,'' Christie said, resting her back against her kitchen chair. She pushed her plate away. ''I'm not really hungry. I'm sorry.'' Lifting her hand, she rubbed the tension in the cords of her neck.

Patrick placed his fork on the edge of his plate and closed his eyes. ''I can barely swallow either.''

Christie fiddled with the napkin she'd dropped beside her plate. ''All we can do is pray.''

''I've been praying all day. I didn't want to leave him there.''

''You had no choice, and you know he's better off.''

He reached across the table and rested his palm

on Christie's hand. "Thanks for being here. It means a lot to me."

"You don't have to thank me, Patrick." He couldn't have kept her away, she had realized as she had waited by his side. Her thoughts drifted now to the small cherub face, the cheeks rosy with fever, his eyes closed or glazed with confusion. The sight squeezed her heart.

"Christie?"

Patrick's voice roused her, and she looked at him, surprised her mind had drifted.

"I realize our thoughts are on Sean right now, but I have a question to ask you." He faltered, lowering his head before raising it again to focus on her. "Something that's been troubling me since yesterday, along with my worries about Sean."

She felt a frown settle on her face, amazed he could think of anything but his child. "What is it?"

"I'd like to know what happened yesterday."

"What do you mean?"

"What happened between us? All of a sudden…"

His voice trailed off as Christie's thoughts struggled back to the conversation that seemed so long ago, yet had only been the day before.

How could she talk about it without letting him know how much she cared? The last thing in the world Christie wanted to do was gain Patrick's pity when he learned his ex-wife had tumbled head over toes again.

"What happened?" he repeated.

She struggled over how to answer him. She'd already said too much the day before, and she didn't want to go there today. "A reality check. That's all."

"A reality check? What does that mean? You told me that you cared. I know you worry whether or not we can make things work. Whether we can let go of the past. All I can say is I feel empty without you and I think you feel the same. Yesterday we were this close," he said lining his index fingers side by side. "This close to resolving issues. This close to being honest about our feelings and fears. This close. Then without an explanation you turned me off. You turned cold."

You turned cold. She'd done it again just as she had years early. When Patrick needed her love and warmth to draw him closer, she'd become aloof and sent him away. She'd slept on her side, facing away from him. Rigid. Unloving. Would this always be the way she handled problems? Fear clouded her reasoning.

"I can't talk about this now. Please." She longed to wrap her arms around him and find some solace against his chest. "I have to think about this, Patrick, and right now all I can think about is Sean."

Patrick's face sagged, and he fell against the seat back. "I'm sorry. It was selfish of me to ask you now. Just know that I want…more than friendship. I want you by my side where you should have been all along. I've asked God to forgive me for what I did to you. Now I'm asking you. Please forgive me. I can't ask you to forget, but maybe someday the hurt will fade. Can you trust me, Christie?''

Tears welled in her eyes. Trust? The one thing she couldn't promise, not after hearing him say he wanted her as a mother for Sean. What about loving her as a wife? Her mind rattled with questions. Did he love her for herself? So often she thought he did. Then, moments came when she knew he didn't.

"Trust is difficult," she said finally. "I'm trying to do that. Trying with all my heart."

"That's all I can ask," he said, sadness flooding his face.

"No. You can ask me to be with you through Sean's illness."

He lifted his downcast eyes. "Will you?"

"Yes. That, I can promise."

Chapter Sixteen

Before visiting hours began Saturday morning, Patrick and Christie rode the elevator to Sean's room. Patrick hesitated outside the door, seeing a doctor hovering above Sean.

He gave a rap and stepped inside, his gaze riveted on Sean's mottled face. "Is something wrong?" He stopped at the edge of the bed while Christie clutched his arm.

The doctor—one Patrick had never seen before—turned to face him. "Are you the boy's father?" the physician asked.

"Yes," he said, extending his hand.

The doctor grasped it in a firm shake.

Noticing the man's serious face, Patrick's pulse jolted. "What's wrong?"

"Your boy's not doing as well as we'd hoped."

"What happened?" Patrick asked, hearing his voice raise in pitch.

"He had a seizure early this morning."

"Seizure?" Panic rolled over Patrick like a truck.

"Oh, no." Christie clutched his arm in a vicelike grip. "What kind of seizure? What's—"

"It was minor. It's caused by the fever. We're waiting for the report on the culture so we can ascertain the most effective medication for this particular bacteria."

Anger charged past Patrick's panic. "Where's Dr. Kedar?"

"He'll be in later this afternoon." The doctor stepped back and regulated the IV drip. "Your son will be fine. Seizures happen occasionally with high fevers. It's nothing to worry about."

"Nothing to worry about. That's easy for..." Patrick felt Christie's fingers press into his arm, and he lowered his voice.

"I'll call the lab again," the doctor said as he headed through the doorway.

Patrick stood frozen to the spot. Fear and frustration tore through him as his gaze shot to Sean, lying deathly quiet, his arms bound to the bed. Patrick jabbed at the straps. "I know this is for his safety, but I hate this."

"He'd pull the needle out if they didn't do something, Patrick." She wrapped her arms around his waist from behind, and he could see her looking at Sean around his back.

Her touch filled him with hope, and he pivoted to face her. Tears pooled in her eyes and rolled down her cheeks. Patrick gathered her into his arms, and she pressed her head against his chest, silent tears turning to soft sobs. He found comfort for himself in her sorrow and rested his cheek against her hair, drawing in the lemony scent of her shampoo and a whisper of sweet perfume.

He held her close, turning so his gaze lingered over his child's face, mottled by fever and sickness. "Pray with me, Christie."

She nodded and lifted her chin to face him.

"Heavenly Father," Patrick said, his voice hushed, "keep Sean in your loving care and bring him back to full health, if it's Your will." He said the last four words, then sent a counter thought. "And please, Lord, let it be Your will."

"Amen," Christie said, easing away to move nearer to Sean. She leaned over the bed railing and kissed his cheek.

Patrick's emotions overflowed. Her compassion for his son rocked him to the core. No matter what she said in words, he knew the truth through her actions. And that's all he needed to know.

Christie moved aside and sank into a chair beside the bed. Patrick pulled another near hers, and they sat in silence, waiting for the doctor, waiting for Sean to open his eyes. His tiny chest rose and fell in uneven breaths, and Patrick returned to his prayer, this time silently.

When he refocused, his gaze settled on Christie's face. Strain and anguish pulled at her features as he knew they did on his own. If nothing more, this horrible situation shed light on his situation with Christie. He needed her, not for Sean, but for himself.

His thoughts settled on First Corinthians. God's description of love. *Love is patient, love is kind. It always protects, always trusts, always hopes, always perseveres. Love never fails.* He'd gone wrong years ago. He'd been impatient and unkind. He'd lacked trust and hope. He'd failed miserably, but not today. Today he knew what love was, not just from God's Word, but in his heart.

Christie knew it, too. Perhaps she always had, and he'd not given her a chance.

Patrick riveted his gaze to his son while moisture welled in his eyes. Sean looked so helpless, so small, so lifeless. His chest lifted and fell with each raspy breath. If he could, Patrick would willingly take the illness from his son and give it to himself.

"We have to think positively," he said, surprised to hear himself speak aloud.

Christie reached over and touched his hand, drawing it to her face still damp with tears. She pressed her cheek against his knuckles, then kissed his fingers.

When she drew his hand away, he met her gaze. "Thanks for being here," he said. "I can live with this rather than not have you at all."

A jaw muscle twitched with his falsehood. Patrick had wanted more. No matter what had happened before, he wanted Christie again. He believed he would never find a woman more beautiful, inside and out. Her lovely face and slender frame tempted him, but more than that, she had a special spirit— generous and caring, sometimes too independent, too unbendable.

But he could live with that by harnessing his own need to control. These were attributes he'd never noticed in Christie years ago. Then she'd keep her feelings inside, afraid to let her needs show until they turned to bitterness.

But she'd lost her bitterness over the past weeks. She was still unbendable at times, but that's what made her Christie. Spunk and spirit. He loved both sides of her. He had to face it. The day she'd admitted her part in their failed marriage and walked away had been one of the loneliest days of his life.

Looking at Christie now lifted his morale. With her hand enveloped in his, he counted the minutes until he heard footsteps. This time, Dr. Kedar entered the room.

Patrick leaped up. "I thought you wouldn't be here until later today."

"My plans changed," he said, moving to Sean's side. He listened through the stethoscope and checked Sean's pulse. "Sean has bacterial pneumonia along with a staph infection. We're changing the antibiotic to Vancomycin. That will make all the difference. You'll have a new boy in a couple of days.'' He grasped Patrick's shoulder and gave it a squeeze. ''I'm sorry. Until we get the lab tests, we do the best we can.''

''He'll be fine?'' Patrick asked.

''Perfect. The new med is on the way.''

''Thank you,'' Christie said.

Patrick nodded, sliding his arm around Christie's waist and drawing strength from her presence. With the Lord and Christie at his side, Patrick knew his life was on the mend.

Monday afternoon Christie pulled into the hospital parking lot. The day at Loving Care had dragged until she could scream. With her thoughts on Sean, she longed to be with Patrick at the hospital.

She hurried inside and took the elevator up to the fourth floor. At Sean's doorway, she stopped, amazed to find her parents at his bedside. ''What are you doing here?''

''Same as you,'' Emma said. ''We're worried about the boy.''

''How is he?''

''Doing better,'' Wes said. ''The fever's coming down.''

Relief washed over her. ''Praise God.'' She gripped her father's arm. He shifted and wrapped it around her shoulder, giving her a hug. Her gaze took in the room. ''Where's Patrick?''

"We sent him down for some coffee. The poor boy needed a break," Emma said.

Christie moved closer, noticing Sean's eyelids flutter, then open. Her heart swelled at the sight.

"Chwistie," Sean said, his voice as soft as a breeze.

"Hi, pal," she said, drawing closer and clasping his tiny hand in hers. "Feeling better?"

He gave her a faint nod.

Christie studied the child's face. His mottled look had faded to ivory with small rosy patches on his cheeks. The perspiration she'd witnessed days earlier had vanished.

"Water," he said, shifting his head to look toward the tray nearby.

Christie eyed the IV still in his arm. "Can he drink liquids?"

Her mother handed her a paper cup with a straw. "The nurse said tiny sips."

Christie cupped his head in her hand and lifted him until the straw met his lips. She lowered him again, set the cup aside and leaned down to kiss his cheek.

"I yove you, Chwistie," he said.

She harnessed the emotion that pressed against her eyes. "I love you, too, Sean."

Turning to hide her tears, Christie stepped away. She had to gain control otherwise she would scare the child.

Her mother grasped her hand and gave it a pat.

"Sean's doing well. Why don't you go down and find Patrick?"

She took another look at the boy before heading through the doorway. Amazed at the feelings that washed over her, Christie calmed herself in the hallway before taking the elevator to the first floor and turning toward the cafeteria.

When she came through the doorway, she bypassed the food stations and made her way into the dining room. Patrick sat alone, his back to her. She had to stop herself from running to him. When she reached him, she felt tears well in her eyes as she smiled in happiness. "He looks so much better."

Patrick rose and took her hands in his. "I'm so relieved."

"I know," she said.

He pulled out a chair, and she sat, her fingers wrapped in his.

"I was surprised to see my parents up there, but I'm not sure why. They're crazy about Sean."

Patrick smiled, realizing she was too, but he wouldn't push. Not anymore. "I know they are. You have good parents. Really special people."

"Thanks," Christie said. "They are. And how's your dad doing? I'm sure it's hard on him to be stuck at home."

"I told him I'd bring him up if Sean doesn't get home soon. But it looks as if he will."

"Really? When?"

"Dr. Minkin was in a little while ago and said if

he keeps improving he can go home in a couple of days. Wednesday, he told me.''

''Wednesday. That'll be something to celebrate.''

He glanced at his watch, checking the date. ''Speaking of celebrating, your birthday's in a few days.''

She shook her head. ''I'm too old for birthdays. Thirty-six is nothing to celebrate.''

''Sure it is. We have two things to be happy about.''

''Three things,'' she said, her face filling with emotion.

''Three?''

''I have to tell you something,'' Christie said.

''Tell me something?''

''It's about Sean.'' She wove her fingers between Patrick's and cupped them with her other hand. ''I've tried to push him away. You know that. I'm constantly reminding myself he's your son and another woman's child. I can't say I'm free from resentment, but these past days, seeing him this way, I don't care whose child Sean is. He's an innocent beautiful boy, and I love him, Patrick.''

Tears misted her smiling eyes—tears of happiness and revelation, Patrick knew. Joy sprang to his heart, hearing her words, and he leaned toward her and kissed her cheek. ''Thank you,'' he whispered.

Though he'd seen her compassion and tenderness long before she would admit it, hearing the words wrapped him in a soothing balm. *Thank You, Lord.*

He sent his praise heavenward, knowing God was in charge and all things happened for His purpose, just as Emma had reminded him.

Patrick stood in the living-room doorway, watching his father play with Sean. All his prayers had been answered, and though Sean was still a little peaked, his energy was back and he'd run around the house as he had before he became ill. Seeing his father in good spirits with color in his face was another gift that the Lord had given him.

Patrick thought back to the troubles in his life. He'd not handled them well, and he couldn't excuse them away. Yes, a mother was important. He'd missed having one, but he'd allowed the absence of a female in his life to let him give way to morbid fears and noxious doubts that had grown into monsters.

Hope. Patience. Forgiveness. The Lord had led him back to the living, and in the past months, he'd begun to feel whole again. Whole and ready to move ahead.

"Are you sure you can handle this boy, Dad?" he asked from the doorway.

"Sure as sunshine. We'll take care of each other."

"I take care of Gwanpa," Sean said, grinning from his pile of blocks on the floor.

"Then I'll see you later." Patrick stepped forward and gave Sean a squeeze. "You be good."

"I be good," he said.

Patrick grabbed his jacket and headed to his car, his feet sliding into the ruts of the frozen earth. He started the engine, then pulled the scraper from the back seat and chiseled at the ice beneath the crusty snow. Finished, he climbed in and rubbed his hands together, appreciating the heater's warmth.

He'd asked Christie to house-hunt with him today, and she'd agreed. His heart skipped as he thought about the day. He'd found a place he liked not too far away from his dad's and close enough to town for convenience. His only hope was that Christie liked it, too.

She was ready when he backed into her driveway. She waved from the doorway, and in a heartbeat, slid beside him before he could be a gentleman and open the door for her.

"Ready?" he asked, feeling a grin fill his face.

"You look like the cat who ate the canary," she said. "What have you got up your sleeve?"

"Nothing," he said, pulling his jacket sleeves open and shaking his arms. "Empty."

She laughed, and Patrick's stomach tightened as he felt amazement at his joy in their relationship now that it had become a solid friendship. Hope. Patience. Forgiveness. The words rang in his head like a litany.

As he drove, he described what he wanted in a house to Christie, hoping his needs were hers.

"You already know what you want. Why do you need me?" she asked.

He ignored her question and pulled up in front of the house for sale. The realtor met him at the door.

When they stepped inside, Christie paused. "It's lovely, Patrick." She headed for the stone fireplace, its broad mantel flanked by two windows that looked out to a landscaped lawn. "You'll have to hire Annie's husband to be your landscaper."

"I already thought of that," he said, beckoning her into the next room.

The realtor waited in the living room while they toured the house—dining room, large family kitchen, four bedrooms, and a family room with space for a computer desk.

"What do you think?" Patrick asked.

"I love it. It has the charm of an older house, yet it's been modernized. It's perfect."

"Perfect?" He gave her a smile, remembering her need for perfection. "I thought so, too."

She grinned, obviously recognizing his wisecrack.

He closed the distance between them and guided her to the large bay window overlooking the snowy backyard. "I can see a swing and slide in that corner."

"Sean will love it."

"They all will."

"They?" Her gaze caught his as a frown settled on her face. "Who's they?"

"All of the children."

"Do you mean…no," she said.

He nodded. "Yes, that's what I mean." His pulse kicked into a gallop. "That's exactly what I mean."

She pivoted around looking at the family room. "It's wonderful, Patrick, but I don't know. I'm not sure I need all this space."

His heart fell as he watched concern spread across her face.

"But we'll have other children, Christie. I realize you have endo—"

She drew her hands up to her face, her deep laugh filling the silence.

Her action startled him, and he felt a puzzled frown grow on his face. "Don't you understand?"

She peeked at him through her fingers and shook her head. "I thought you wanted me to buy this for Loving Care."

"Loving Care?" He pulled her hands from her face and pulled her closer, wrapping his arms around her waist. "No. I had something else in mind. Us. You and me and Sean and other children—however many God blesses us with."

Tears welled in her eyes. "You want to buy this home for us." She placed her hand over her heart, then laid her other palm against his chest, feeling his heart beat as wildly as her own.

"If you'll have us." He searched her eyes for an answer, a prayer rising. "I love you, Christie. I never stopped. I just veered off course a little."

"You said you believed the Lord did things for

His purpose. I believe that. He's had us in His loving care for so long just waiting for the day to bring us back together again.''

"Then, you mean yes?'' Patrick said, holding her so close he felt her heart beating against his.

She raised her hands and cradled his face in her palms. "Yes, with all my heart.''

His lips met hers, soft and warm, like coming home. He held her close, remembering so many things they shared—her frame fitting against him like the piece of a puzzle lost but now found.

Her soft sigh greeted his ears, and he deepened the kiss, knowing that trust took time, but they had God on their side. Everything would be all right from now on.

"Happy birthday, dear Christie. Happy birthday to you.''

Christie grinned, seeing her parents standing around the Hanuman table singing "Happy Birthday.'' Sean's healthy presence added to her joy.

Christie blew out the candles with Sean's help. He giggled, and she gave him a big hug, loving the feel of the child in her arms. If he was all God planned for her, she could live with that. God saw the bigger picture. She saw only a shadow of what was to come.

"So, cut the cake already.'' Wes said.

Christie took the knife and measured out the slices while Patrick dug into the ice cream carton and plopped a scoop onto the plate for those who wanted it.

When the last piece was ready, Patrick lifted his plate in the air. "Before we fork into this cake, I have a birthday toast to make."

"Hear! Hear!" his father said, raising his dish. "I've never toasted with cake, but there's always a first time."

"Where's my toast," Sean asked, studying the group with a puzzled look.

"Not toast from bread, Sean. This means a good wish."

"A birfday wish?" Sean asked.

"Something like that." Patrick tousled his hair and lifted his plate. "To Christie, who's found her way back into my life. May God bless us in the years to come with complete happiness in our new lives together."

Plates hung suspended in the air while their parents looked from one to the other with puzzled expressions.

"Does this mean...?" Emma asked.

"It means Christie has agreed to be my wife... again," Patrick said.

Their startled silence become a clatter of good wishes, hugs and kisses. Christie's eyes glistened with tears, and she hoisted Sean into her arms from his high chair and gave him a hug.

"So when's the big day?" Wes asked, shaking Patrick's hand until Christie feared it would fall off.

"We decided not to wait," Christie said. "We're getting married New Year's Eve."

Patrick slid his arm around her shoulder, cherishing every moment together. "It seemed appropriate. A new year and a new beginning."

"I'm so happy," Emma said, tears running down her smooth cheeks. "God's answered my prayer."

Christie grinned. "After all your lectures?" She gave Sean a squeeze and shifted him into Patrick's arms.

Patrick held Sean against his chest, praising God for the miracles—his father's good health, Sean's recovery and Christie's love.

Wes gave them a knowing grin. "You know your mother. She lectures and then she prays."

Chuckles filled the room until Joe stepped forward and gave Christie a bear hug. "I couldn't be happier. You were always a good daughter-in-law, and I'm grateful God's seen fit to bring you two back together."

"Amen to that," Emma said. She moved closer to Sean. "Do you understand, Sean? Your daddy is going to marry Christie."

"We've been practicing," Patrick said. He nuzzled his son against his chin before giving Sean a nod.

The child giggled, then drew in a deep breath. "Chwistie is gonna be my new mommy."

Patrick looked at his son with pride, then at the others who stood around them with misted eyes.

Nothing—not the past or the losses he'd experience—nothing could hold back the complete joy that he felt.

"I love you," Christie whispered. "Both of you, with all my heart."

Chapter Seventeen

The band played a love song, and Christie swayed in Patrick's arms. Through the window of the Bay Breeze dining room, she could see lights flicker on the frozen shore of the lake. In moments, fireworks would ring in the new year.

The song ended, and Patrick guided her off the dance floor, then excused himself to get her a drink, looking handsome in his dark suit and tie.

Jemma stepped to her side and grasped her hand. "Your wedding was beautiful. Simple, but elegant."

"Thanks," Christie said, still amazed that she and Patrick were husband and wife once more. "I'm so glad Philip let us use the resort for our little reception."

"He'd have it no other way." She kissed Christie's cheek, but before she moved off, Patrick reappeared with a drink and dangled a key.

"What's that?"

"The penthouse suite."

"Penthouse?"

Jemma laughed. "It was our living quarters before we moved. Now, Philip uses it for special occasions. It's our gift to you."

"Gift?" Christie said, eyeing Jemma then Patrick.

He nodded. "Philip just gave me the key. He's canceled our regular room."

Before Christie could respond, a boom rolled across the sky, and she turned to the wall of windows, looking out on the lake and seeing the flash of color like fairy dust spiraling into the water. From the shore, fireworks burst into the sky. Neon chrysanthemums—pink and yellow petals—drifted downward to the dark water.

The band segued into "Auld Lang Syne," and as the people sang, moving together in groups and sharing happy-new-year wishes, Patrick moved to Christie's side, folding her into his arms and holding her close. She wanted nothing more. She closed her eyes, tears blurring her vision, praying that if she never had another child, Patrick would not grieve the loss. He loved children and deserved them.

"You're beautiful," Patrick whispered into her ear, swaying with the music, their eyes focused on the firework sky. "My promise today is solid, Christie. I want you to know that. I won't let you down again.''

"Till death do us part," she said, feeling confident in their matured love. "I trust you, Patrick."

"Those are the sweetest words," he said. "You'll always be in my loving care, just as the Lord has watched over us.''

His lips touched hers, tender yet urgent. She gave of herself, moving her mouth against his, loving the feel and taste of his lips. His hands caressed her back and one moved up her arm and captured her cheek. "This is loving," he whispered, his lips beside hers, "and this is what hope and patience promises."

She looked at him through her tears, joy filling her heart.

A jingle drew her eyes downward.

The key to the penthouse.

With her mind whirling, she stepped back and bumped into a waiter's tray. Napkins and silverware tumbled fo the floor. She grinned and bent down to retrieve them, but Patrick had bent down first. Their hands touched as they reached for the same fork, and her mind sailed back to months earlier in the pharmacy.

Patrick cupped her hand in his. "Haven't we met somewhere before?"

She nodded, her heart thundering with the remembrance.

Patrick rose and took her hand to help her rise.

He gathered the napkins and silverware and dropped them on the tray. "Ready?"

She nodded, her heart ready to explode. Ready? Yes. Ready to open her heart and arms, to give of herself and never hold back again. God had opened her eyes to the true meaning of love—a love that forgives, a love that endures hardships, a love that never ends.

Patrick guided her across the floor, saying goodbye as they exited. In the hall, they moved down the corridor to the penthouse elevator, pushed the button, and when the door opened they stepped inside, their lives woven as tightly together as their fingers.

Patrick's hand trembled as he turned the key in the lock. The door swung open to an elegant foyer and ahead of them, a stretch of windows letting in the night sky and the fireworks finale.

They stood a moment, watching the last ember drop into the dark water, then made their way down another hallway to the master suite.

Patrick noted that Philip had sent up their luggage. He'd thought of everything. Two fluted glasses sat on the night stand beside a bottle of sparkling fruit juice. He uncorked the bottle and filled the goblets, then offered Christie hers. When she grasped the stem, he raised his glass. "This is to us. To a new beginning. To a blessed life."

She took a sip and moved forward, her soft pink gown shining with iridescent beads.

He set his flute on the night stand and drew her into his arms. Their lips met, fitting as perfectly together as if they were meant to be.

She eased back and gazed into his eyes with a shyness he hadn't expected.

''Go ahead,'' he said, tilting his head toward the bathroom. ''You first.''

She snapped open her luggage and drew out a rustle of white filmy cloth, so gossamer it took Patrick's breath away. He remembered their first wedding night filled with innocent intimacy. Tonight was no different.

With his back to the door, Patrick stared into the night sky. The Lord had provided His own fireworks—a full moon and a sparkling array of stars. He found the north star, a small steady light that guided sailors home. Tonight he was home.

He heard the door open, and Christie stepped into the room. She glided toward him like a dream—a dream he'd had since the day they met in the pharmacy.

He opened his arms to her, feeling the slippery cloth beneath his hands. He drew his palm down her arm. God had given him the gift. The Lord had meant them to be husband and wife, and his sin was washed clean in God's saving grace.

''Patrick,'' she said, her voice as soft as a whisper.

He kissed her hair and waited.

"I don't want to disappoint you. I know you want more children, and I can't promise—"

"We made one promise today, my love. To have and to hold from this day forward. That's all the promise I need."

"But…I'd love to have a child. You know that," she said. "A playmate for Sean."

"I didn't say we wouldn't try, Christie. I'm here. You're here. God's beside us, and with his blessing, miracles can happen."

His lips met hers, and with his kiss, he sealed the promise. What more could he ask? God's blessing had brought him home to Loving, had brought Christie's love back into his life. His prayer rose. *Lord, I ask one more blessing, but this one for Christie. A child. A child of her own.*

Like the fireworks that brightened the sky, his heart filled with light as he drew Christie into his arms, his prayer still on his lips and in his heart.

* * * * *

Dear Reader,

When writing *Loving Care,* I gave much thought to the delicate relationship between husband and wife. I was touched by the depth of trust, honesty and faithfulness that is necessary to keep a marriage healthy and solid. Broken trust is like that "cracked plate" Patrick mentions in the story. It is never easily mended.

But we know that the Lord promises to hear our prayers. He alone can mend broken hearts and bind our deepest wounds, and in times when we see no hope, He offers us opportunities and dreams beyond our imagination. Not all marriages can heal like Christie and Patrick's, but with faith and trust in God, all things are possible.

My prayer is that whatever "cracked plate" you hold in your hand, you'll give it to the Lord. Let Him make it like new again.

Gail Gaymer Martin